Damen Goes to Peru

by C.H. Lyn

Miss Belle's Travel Guides Book 2

Content Warning

Violence

Language

As stated in the previous book's content warnings, there are no graphic depictions of SA in these stories. There is mention of trauma related to SA.

Dedication

Tracey -
PSMLP
Love you

Chapter One

Damen

Playing House

Smoke trails from my nostrils. My body, my skin and muscles, the places that have been cold and tight and not myself since my last assignment, return to the me I'm used to. Em's warm fingers trace circles across my upper arm, the bronze skin of my chest, following the thin trail of black hair down to the waist of my jeans.

I pass her the joint, and she inhales.

It's not often we get to do this—sit on the little balcony of her studio apartment, watching the sun set over the city as we curl together on the loveseat she picked up off the sidewalk a year ago. Her Jack Skellington blanket keeps our legs warm. A plate of mini cupcakes sits precariously on the edge of the grated metal at our feet; a few more inches and the ceramic would shatter on the asphalt three stories below.

I reach forward and snatch a chocolate covered bite before settling back into the cushions. Em leans into my chest, her dark hair tickling my shoulder.

"How long can you stay this time?"

Her voice is a murmur. A whisper that bypasses my ear, seeping directly into my heart. Gentle vibrations that echo in the chambers of my chest.

She wants me to stay.

I want to stay, too.

"I'm not sure," I reply. After three years in the United States, my accent is still noticeable when I'm not actively trying to hide it. I used to around Em. Our first few encounters I sounded like I grew up here. But over time I slipped into the Peruvian purr she loves so much. I explained away the transition with some half-true words about getting better prices when I use a North American accent. "I don't have another assignment for at least a month."

She lights up, rocketing off my chest to drill those sharp eyes into mine. "A month?"

I shake my head with a chuckle and take a bite of the cupcake. "I won't be able to stay the whole time. I've got other responsibilities." My words are mumbled through the delicate cake melting in my mouth.

She pouts, that bottom lip bringing fire to my stomach and lower.

I swallow and backpedal. "I'll be here a while, Em."

She morphs the pout, her teeth coming out to bite the lip. The fire grows.

"We're going to miss the sunset if you keep looking at me like that," I tell her.

Her grin is almost as sexy as the bite. Her smile grows, filling out her round face. I lean in. My lips brush against hers, gently at first. Always gently at first. There is always the option to pull away without guilt or fear.

She doesn't.

Her kiss consumes me. I forget my last assignment. I forget the pangs of homesickness that plague me. I forget that this beautiful creature before me is Miss Belle's sister.

The joint smokes in the ashtray as we make up for the time I've been gone. Without a word, she rises from the couch and leads me inside. The Skellington blanket falls to the ground, left forgotten with the cupcakes in the cold spring evening.

She draws me into the living room. Low light from a single lamp casts artistic shadows across the multitude of paintings and charcoal sketches hung on the walls.

Em slips off her thin oversized T-shirt and wraps her arms around my neck. Her lips burn under mine. Each nibble of her bottom lip, her neck, her nipple, makes me harder. Each stroke of her fingers across my skin.

Her breasts are full, plump. They fill my hands. Their warmth seeps into me as our chests press against one another.

Em pushes me back, giving a laugh as I fall onto the couch. She pulls off the last of her clothes as I roll a condom on. Her legs straddle me. Her thighs are thick; the pudge of her stomach bumps against me. She is all soft and squishy and sweet, and I sink into her the way one sinks into a feather bed.

When we are both satisfied and buzzing with afterglow, she climbs off my lap and plops sideways onto the couch. Her legs drape over me in a way that brings peace into my heart. I pull them close to my chest, kissing her knees.

I get cleaned up, then return to my seat. Em curls into me and we sit there in a happy, comfortable silence until she falls asleep and I... I drift in my own mind, this time with Em chasing away the regret, the shame, the fear.

Well, chasing most of it away.

Em doesn't know what I do.

In her eyes, I'm an art buyer for a rich and mysterious client. While that's technically true—I do buy art for a rich and mysterious client—it's a cover. A cover for me, so I can travel the world and pretend to be inspecting and collecting art when I'm really sleeping with powerful people to learn their secrets or taking back art which was stolen in the first place. And a cover for Miss Belle, so she can help finance her little sister's career.

Em's been drawing, painting, and creating since she could hold a crayon. Her art is amazing. Stunning and insightful and stuck in a third-rate gallery she's overly loyal to. I'd push for her to move, but there's no point. The Romana gallery accepted her work when she first moved to Brooklyn; she's not leaving them until she graduates next year.

Em pulls a purple striped skirt over her black leggings and flashes a flirty grin at me. I'm not dressed yet. Getting dressed before nine on a Saturday, when I'm on vacation, seems like a betrayal to relaxation.

I wonder what she'd think—Miss Belle, that is—of me and her sister. We've been doing this for almost a year now, though I've been buying her art twice as long. Nothing official. Nothing too real. It can't be, not with me disappearing for months at a time, then popping in to buy artwork and stay with Em for a week. Playing house.

I'd be angry if I were Miss Belle. I'd be furious that I hadn't told her sister the truth yet.

I can't, of course. It would be giving up secrets that don't belong only to me. It would be dangerous. For Em, for Miss Belle, for all of the Guides.

I can't risk it. I can't imagine Miss Belle's fury if I *did* tell her sister the truth about what we do.

That's not true. I *can* imagine her fury. It's not something I ever want to see.

"Damen?"

I snap out of my daze and catch Em staring at me. She's fully dressed now. Flowing sleeves cover the arms she thinks are too jiggly and I think are perfect. Loose ruffles hide the weight on her stomach, the stretch marks I love tracing, the skin I love to kiss.

She's gorgeous. A black and purple force of gothic nature.

She's still talking, I need to pay attention. "Listen, I know you have that rule about not getting dressed before nine, but I'm hungry and I need coffee. Now. You can stay here if you like, but I'm going to your favorite café."

I show her my teeth and wink. "You could always bring something back to me, *bella bonita.*"

Her eye roll is disturbingly like her sister's.

"Nope. If you wanna eat, get your butt out of bed, and come with me."

With a laugh and a groan, I obey. I go to the closet, pulling out a neatly hung pair of black jeans and a wrinkle-free gray button-up. The air outside will be crisp based on the last few mornings. I drape a suit-jacket over my shoulders and finish the look with a pair of dark leather Santonis, an Italian brand I'm fond of.

There is no scruff on my face. I only need to shave once every three or four days to keep my skin smooth. It's both a source of frustration and a convenience. It would be easier to blend in certain places if I were capable of growing a full-length beard, and disguising my look would be a simpler task.

Then again, being barely able to grow peach fuzz makes passing as a teenager to destroy the lives of disgusting old men much easier.

I follow Em out her door, helping to jerk it closed as it sticks on the hinge. The hallway is dark. Most of these lights have been burned out as long as I've known Emily. The few that work flicker.

Mrs. Gacey two doors down sticks her head out at the sound of footsteps and offers us a gummy smile and a "good morning." We return it, and I make a mental note to bring her a bagel after Em starts painting for the day.

We enter the stairwell, and the temperature drops a full five degrees. I wrap my arm around Em's shoulder and pull her close.

Grated metal above and below clanks with each step. There's scrambling at the bottom, and we grin at the half-dozen kids running around the first floor of stairs. They've got a few plastic lids, the heavy-duty kind you'd find at a box-storage store. As I shove open the door to the street, one of them clambers on a lid and launches from the top steps with his makeshift urban sled. Screaming and laughter follow us into the natural morning light.

Brooklyn looks different in the daytime. The glow from the streetlights and setting sun have gone, leaving stark sunlight to bleach the streets clean. I don't mind it—the dirt, the garbage, the occasional sleeping bag in a doorway. It reminds me of home.

Big cities are all the same, whether in the United States, Peru, or anywhere else.

Our usual breakfast joint is a twenty-minute walk. Em holds my hand, telling me about her latest work. We stopped by the gallery displaying her artwork on my first day in town. I want to go back. There's nothing quite like looking at the artwork of someone you—

My phone rings, tinkling filling the air from my pocket. I pull it out with my free hand, and a smile splits across my face.

"Mama?"

"*Alo Mijo*," my mother cheerily greets me. Her voice sends a ripple of warmth through my stomach. She continues in Spanish, "I wanted to call and check on you. Miss Belle says we can talk more, no?"

I swallow and glance at Em. She's grinning. There's no flash of recognition. I'm hoping she can't hear the other end of the conversation. She may not speak fluent Spanish, but it's easy enough to pick out a name. I slide my thumb up the phone and turn down the volume.

"That's right, Mama. How are things in Peru?"

"The cat is pregnant, and Rosie's dog keeps barking in the middle of the night. It's scaring the chickens."

I turn the phone away from my mouth as a chuckle escapes me. "How is Rosie?" I ask when she finishes discussing her concerns about egg laying levels.

"She starts school in two weeks. I don't know how she will handle it. The drive to Arequipa is over an hour away. A bus would be even longer."

"Can she try to find a place to stay in the city?"

"No," Mama snaps. "I don't want her living somewhere far away. Besides, we don't have the money for that."

I frown at both her tone and the words. "Mama, I've been sending you money every month. There should be plenty."

"*Ay Mijo*, I've been saving it for you. When you come home, you can buy yourself a nice house and settle down."

I drop Em's hand, my fingers pressing my forehead just between my eyebrows. I grit my teeth. "You're supposed to be using that money for you, Carmen, and Rosie. I won't be coming home for a long time, Mama."

My gut churns as I say the words. It already has been a long time.

A door slams, and I hear Mama talking to someone else in a muffled voice.

She returns her focus to me and says, "Carmen just got home. You should talk to your sister. Tell her to be home more often."

There's a groan on the other end of the phone. "Mama, can't I set my stuff down?"

I stifle another laugh. I can picture Carmen's exasperated expression as she walks in with an armful of groceries or something and our mother's first move is shoving a phone in her hand.

There's a scuffling sound. "Hey, little brother."

I roll my eyes. "I'm not your little brother."

Beside me, Em snorts.

Carmen laughs on the line. "Well, I was born first, so technically—"

"By five minutes," I burst out. "That doesn't count."

Em's snort morphs into a chuckle. I glare at her.

"Well," my twin stifles a yawn, "I'm taller than you too. So..."

I heave a sigh and stuff my hand into my jacket pocket. "What's new with you? It's been a while."

"—Ha. You don't want to hear about our boring lives. Tell me about your adventures traveling around the world."

There was a falter there. Subtle, but I know my sister, and I heard it. "No, really, tell me what's been going on down there. I miss Peru more than I thought possible when I left."

The bitter streak in my voice makes her sigh. "We miss you too, D. Let's see... Rosie is mad at mom. She wants to get a job in Arequipa so she can pay to stay there while she's taking classes at the University."

"She doesn't need to," I grumble. "That's what the money I send you is for."

"Yeah, but it's not about the money."

My brow furrows as I stare at the sidewalk.

"Mom won't let her get a job or live there. Not after..." Carmen backtracks and starts again. "She just doesn't want Rosie alone in the city."

I falter. Stumble in my steps as Em pulls ahead of me. She pauses and glances back. I wave for her to continue. I'll catch up.

Carmen's unspoken words trigger something I'm barely able to control. My heartbeat thunders, and I take my hand from my pocket to fiddle with the small golden cross dangling from my neck.

I nod and swallow. "I understand. But she can't drive hours every day to get to school."

Something moves behind me, and I jerk my head around. A bike messenger speeds past. A sigh of relief calms my pounding heart.

I inhale a deep breath. The oxygen and the ridges on my cross pressing into my fingers do the trick of easing my nerves. I change the subject. "What about you? Still reading in those villages?"

"Yeah..." There is a hesitation in her voice. She continues in English. "I've actually been working on something new there. There's a company trying to steal the land out from under the Quechua people. A couple villages right along the Amazon. We're protesting."

The chain of my cross rubs against my neck as I pull it back and forth. "Are you being careful? Protesting can be dangerous."

Her half-laugh is followed by an irritated, "Really? You're telling me to be careful after the last three years?"

"That's different." I lower my voice, my gaze on Em as she turns to walk backward ahead of me, raising her eyebrow and gesturing pointedly to her side. "I got training. I can handle myself."

"Excuse me?"

The sharp edge to her voice makes me wince. I probably shouldn't have said that.

"I can handle myself too. Just fine. I'm not the one—" she breaks off again, but I know what she was going to say.

She's not the one who had to flee Peru three years ago.

"I know, Car. I'm sorry." I heave a sigh and jog to catch up to Em. "I miss you guys. I miss Peru. *Dios*, it would be enough just to see the mountains again, you know? Or the shoreline."

"It's safer for you there."

"I know," I grumble. "But it's been long enough." I reach Em and slide my fingers between hers again. "We were talking," I speak carefully again, "and I think I'll be able to come out to spend Christmas with the family."

"I—near Christmas? Yeah, that's a good idea."

"Listen, I have to go."

Beside me, Em shakes her head emphatically. She points to the phone and mouths, "It's okay; take your time."

I plant a kiss on her head.

"Me too," Carmen says. "I just finished packing up the car and I have to leave soon. Mama," she pauses for emphasis, I assume to glare at our mother, "keeps telling me to stay another day. But I have to get back."

"Yeah, listen, I get you're doing a protest, but try to keep your head down, *claro*?"

"Right, miss you too, D." Her distracted voice fades from the phone. There's a muffled "*te amo*," and she passes the phone to our mother.

It takes a few more minutes to get off the phone. Mama tears up when I tell her I might be able to come visit near Christmas. She's excited we may be able to go to Christmas Day Mass together. I am too.

Em grins as I slide my phone back into my pocket. "That sounds like it went well. You might be visiting your family this year?"

I nod. I can't tell Em much, but she does know it's been difficult not seeing my family for a while.

She asks questions, and I answer. Telling her about my sisters. About the village our father was from, the town I grew up in, the foods and sights I miss the most.

A few minutes later, we arrive at our restaurant.

I hold the door. Susana, our favorite waitress and the one who works the morning shift six days a week, flashes a grin from the hostess stand. She gestures to our usual table in the far corner.

I sidle into the booth seat with the wall at my back and a good view of both the front and kitchen doors. The TV in the corner runs through the morning news. The volume is low, subtitles scrawling across the bottom of the screen.

The diner is mostly empty. An older man sits at the bar nursing a black coffee and a blueberry muffin. There's a huddle of teenagers at the window. They've pulled two tables together and now eagerly suck down frozen coffee drinks.

A flash of memory hits me. Well, more a feeling really. Being that young. Not that 23 is very old, so I suppose being that carefree.

"So, these responsibilities you have..." Em leans into her elbows, hands on either side of her face, and stares at me. "How long before you leave to deal with them?"

I shrug. At the same time, I pull my phone from my pocket and check it for messages from Miss Belle. She and Missa give me time, a lot of time, to recuperate after an assignment like the one I had with Prentice. Having sex with homophobic old men who enjoy the company of those much younger than themselves is not an aspect of my job I find enjoyable.

Though the consequences for every gay person in the United States—and the legality of their marriages—was well worth my discomfort.

"I don't know, *bella*." I feign hurt. "Do you want me gone? Am I boring you already?"

She shoves my arm and sticks out a playful tongue. "No. But I don't want to go to class Monday and come home to find you've disappeared again."

"As I promised last time, if I have to leave suddenly again, I will call or at least send you a message about it."

Susana comes over with menus but doesn't put them down. "Know what y'all want?"

I order the pancakes. Blueberry with the real maple syrup and a side of bacon. Em gets a breakfast burrito and a side of potatoes, extra crispy.

Susana pours coffee into mugs, sets down a bowl of honey packets and a cylinder of cream, and heads toward the kitchen with a smile. She didn't write down our order. Something tells me the cook is already frying up my bacon. We've gotten the same thing every day for the last week.

Em pulls a sketchbook and a zippered pencil case from her bag. With the top of her foot pressed up against my calf for comfort, she flashes me another grin and ducks her head. Dark hair dangles down. Her fingers twitch across the paper.

I settle into the cushions behind me and go back and forth between people watching and checking out the international news channel Susana likes putting on. Steam rises in the mug before me. I pour in copious amounts of honey and cream and let it cool while I gaze blankly at the newscasters.

A name slides across the bottom of the screen. I blink.

The unease in my stomach, a constant presence that rarely dissipates, grows.

I must be wrong because the news story on the screen doesn't match up with the name.

Buccero can't be opening a new office in Lima, Peru. He's rotting in a jail cell. The one I helped put him in three years ago. It must have been a different name, a different city they are talking about.

In my peripheral vision I catch Em glancing up at me as I stand. The camera angle on the TV pans. Lima is lit up like a dazzling array of stars. Cars, pressed together and ignoring traffic lines, zoom down the highway. I recognize these buildings, these parks. I recognize the business district where the camera slows to a stop.

Em says something I don't catch, but I stride forward rather than asking her to repeat it. When I reach the bar, I murmur for Susana to turn up the volume. She raises an eyebrow but obliges.

Buccero Vincente. It's his name. I'm looking for it, and I catch it this time, scrawled across the screen. My heart thuds against my chest with an aching rapidity. Nerves like lightning buzz down my spine. Fury clouds my mind.

Pain wraps tendril-like fingers around my stomach and squeezes the breath out of me. The burning in my gut is familiar. It is a sensation that has never quite left me, even when I thought he was gone—about thirty seconds ago.

I'm snapped out of it as the image on the television changes. This interview is more recent than the stock footage they were using before. The sun shines down onto a multi-story office building in the heart of Lima. A young man stands in front of a crystal fountain.

He is a boy. Eighteen or nineteen at the most. His hair is slicked back – like mine used to be. His suit is tailored to his body. He smiles into the camera, hands clasped before him as he answers questions.

English subtitles glide across the screen. I ignore them.

The boy, Arturo, laughs off what could be a tense question. "No, no, no. I assure you, Señor Vincente thinks of his time in jail as a retreat of sorts. He was allowed much needed time to himself. To reflect on his business, the direction he wishes it to go, and the wonderful plans he has to help build up all of Peru. You must know how my employer loves our beautiful country. He could have fled the false charges placed against him three years ago, but his love for our home was too strong." He shakes his hands as though washing away a bad memory.

"Let's not dwell on the past. Señor Vincente did not ask you all here today to discuss what has already happened, rather to tell you about the future in store for our glorious country. This building," he gestures to the towering structure behind him, "is the new point of operations for Señor Vincente's company. The shareholders and board have been running things smoothly these past few years, but now is the time for growth, development, and expansion. The outright purchase of this gem of Lima is a symbol for those who doubt Señor Vincente's return to..."

He pauses, and I know he was going to say power. I know it from the pit in my gut to the blood boiling in my veins.

"... his position at the company."

My hands are shaking. Hands, lips, the very atoms of my being. This is impossible. This cannot be happening.

But then it does happen. A figure comes onto the screen, and the sound of thunder slams into my ears. I am blind and deaf and stunned to everything except the face of the man who tortured me for two years.

The man who ought to be rotting in a prison cell.

I joined Miss Belle to put him away for life. To get justice.

But Buccero's smile is as white as ever. His skin the caramel color of those native to the coastal regions of Peru. His suit costs more than Em's rent in downtown Brooklyn.

He clasps a hand on Arturo's shoulder, and I recognize the look he gives his assistant.

Bile pools in my throat.

My chest heaves. I clench my jaw, refusing to throw up the remains of cupcakes and coffee. The ringing in my ears fades as Buccero jovially answers questions.

Arturo has done well picking this group of reporters. None of them ask about his time in prison. None mention the rumors that circulated three years ago, the rumors that had nothing to do with the corporate fraud and tax evasion he was imprisoned for.

A hand touches my arm. I yank backward, jerking to the side and staring around for an enemy.

There is none. Only Em, her wide eyes fearful and confused by my reaction.

"I'm sorry; I'm…" I can't finish my thought. Buccero is still on the screen. She turns to watch the television with me and, with her by my side, I'm able to detach from my nightmare brought to life.

Arturo hands Buccero a shining pair of golden scissors. The older man – I feel a rush of momentary happy vengeance at the way prison has aged him – slices through a ribbon blocking the glass doors leading into an impressive looking lobby.

The news segment switches to a blonde woman behind a desk and while she continues to talk about Buccero's company, my focus drains away.

I'm still in New York. Standing in a diner with a woman who cares for me at my side, expecting me to be here with her for a week at least. Because that's what I promised.

My heart sinks, but as it does it collides with the rage building in my stomach and my plan is resolved. I have a go-bag prepared. It's waiting in the hotel Miss Belle booked for me. The one she books for me every time I visit Em. The one I only use to store things Em is better off not knowing about.

"I have to go."

"What?" Em pulls on my arm, and I turn to look at her.

Susana stares at the two of us with wide eyes.

Em tugs me toward our table, and I follow as my thoughts career from plan to plan, fast approaching what I know must be done.

"What do you mean you have to go? I thought you didn't have anything new for a while?" She is hurt. Hurt and confused and disappointed.

I swallow, sinking down and reaching for my coffee mug with one hand, my phone with the other. "I'm sorry, Em. Really, I am. But there is something I need to take care of. Please believe me when I tell you it is important."

I pull up JFK, find the next available flight to Peru, and book it. Em watches me the whole time, using the patience God didn't give her sister to wait until I'm giving her my full attention. When I set the phone down and lift the mug to my lips with shaking hands, she speaks.

"I don't want it to be like this, Damen. I don't want us to share a few nights, and then I don't hear from you for weeks."

"You don't like the nights we share?" I ask the unfair question because I know it is unfair. I hope it will change the direction of this conversation. Maybe I'm even hoping for a fight. A way for her to not miss me the way I will miss her while I am gone.

But intelligence is a gift God gave both Em and Miss Belle. She raises an eyebrow at me, clicks her tongue against the roof of her mouth, and settles back in her chair.

"I'm not going to bother answering that."

I sigh. "My flight leaves tomorrow morning."

"Where are you going?" She gestures to the television which Susana has turned back down. "To Peru? Why? It can't have anything to do with buying art because you didn't get any notice from your boss."

"Em." I put my hands on the table, and she follows suit. I take her fingers in mine. I squeeze. "I cannot answer your questions today. I don't know if I can answer them tomorrow, but I want to. I want this to be more than what it has been. I promise I will call you, and message you, as often as I can while I'm gone."

Her face flickers through a range of emotions before it finally settles – to my relief – on begrudging contentment.

I leave the phone she knows about at home when I go on missions. I take my work phone. The one designed to get service almost anywhere on the planet. The one that has exactly three numbers programmed into it and doesn't show a number when it calls someone. But this isn't a sanctioned mission; bringing my normal phone won't be a problem.

She squeezes my hands back. "You've got till tomorrow?"

I nod.

"So... we can finish breakfast?" A glimmer of the grin that sets my soul on fire flashes across her face, but the confusion and worry linger.

I want to stay. To ease her mind with kisses and chocolate and being together. But I have a debt to repay – a debt I didn't realize was still on the books – but a debt nonetheless.

I squeeze her hand and tell her yes.

We will finish breakfast, spend the day together. Then tomorrow, I will pack up my things and take my go-bag from the hotel. I will fly to my home, to Peru, where I haven't been for three long years.

And I will kill Buccero Vincente.

People will tell you to experience as much as possible when you travel. Try a new restaurant every day, order food you've never tasted, never get something you can get back home. That's a load of crap.

Here's why: it'll drain you. Finding a new place to eat every day? Trying something your stomach and tongue might not enjoy for each meal? Nah.

Should you try new things? Absolutely.

If you find something you like, are you allowed to go back? Of course!

There are a handful of restaurants in a handful of cities that are go-tos. If you find a coffee shop around the corner from your hostel, feel the freedom to order your pumpkin chai latte every morning of your trip. Maybe find something new for dinner, but don't pigeon-hole yourself into overexerting your limit for brand new experiences.

There's also nothing quite like becoming besties with a barista you'll only know for a week.

Chapter Two
Miss Belle
Coffee and a Proposal

It's early. Early morning in Chicago where the word "spring" seems to have been forgotten. I shiver in my light jacket, which was plenty warm in New York, thank you very much. Missa snickers from her seat next to me on the firm taxi cushions.

"What?" I snap.

"Cold?"

My eyelids half-close in a fierce glare. "Shaddup."

"I told you to bring a proper coat." Her voice is smug, sitting there in a thick, navy-blue wool jacket, jeans, brown boots, and a cream-colored scarf with matching gloves.

Meanwhile, I'm freezing my ass off in a comfortable T-shirt and thin zip-up. I pull the hood over my head, face the window, and ignore her.

She chuckles again.

I focus on the road, the houses and businesses we rush past. Missa and I caught the earliest flight to Chicago. The new girl, Delilah, has been with Erin for about a week now, and it's well past time for the welcome speech.

We stop at a red light, and I watch a storefront owner sweep off the sidewalk in front of his bakery. The broom scoots back and forth, back and forth. An identical movement leaps through my memory and images flash across my mind. Green vegetation, little shops opening up as the sun rises over the mountains and tires rumble against pavement, the weight of metal, the feel of a rubber grip clenched in my hand.

I glance down at my right hand. My knuckles are white, my fingers latched around the door handle. My left hand, resting on my leg, trembles.

Something grabs my arm, and I jump, heart racing. Missa stares at me, her hand resting on my shoulder, concern clouding her eyes.

I turn away from her, press my head against the seat, and close my eyes. I will my fingers to relax. After a moment, I can move my hand from the door and tuck it under my thigh. Each breath I take is purposeful. Inhale... exhale... inhale... exhale... over and over. Just breathe.

I rub a finger across the pale pink flesh beginning to scar above my left eye. Just a graze, but it has left a small divot in my forehead. Not all that visible, but I can feel it.

The cab pulls to the curb in front of an ancient, three-story brick house. The garden is greener than last time I was here. Erin hasn't planted any of the new veggies yet–there is still a promise of freezes in the near future–but the rains Chicago has been getting have made the plants left-over from last year explode in a chorus of color.

Missa pulls a wad of cash from the pocket of her "proper" coat and passes it up to the driver. He says... something. I'm not listening. I climb out of the car, open the little wrought-iron gate, and head up the walkway.

"Hey," Missa calls. She takes a few quick steps with those insanely long legs and is right next to me. Her fingers curl around my arm, gentle but firm as she stops me from continuing toward the door. "Are you okay?"

My gaze flicks past her face, staring at a purple flower a little way behind her. I could lie. But me lying to Missa is akin to a dog trying to lie about digging through the garbage. I wouldn't be fooling anyone.

"I just... I had a moment." I purse my lips, hoping that's enough.

"What happened?"

Of course it's not enough. I should know better. "It was just... it was... something reminded me of Thailand and I..." I swallow, my words sticking in my throat. A heavy, angry breath dives in and out of my chest. I flex my fingers, calming my breathing and my heartbeat. "I had a moment. That's all."

She stares at me, her blue eyes boring into my green ones. A long time passes, and then she nods. Her slender arms gently wrap around my torso. She holds me for a minute, waiting for me to pull away first. It takes a little while; I don't want to give up the warm comfort there, the feeling that the pounds of pressure weighing me down have been lifted. Even if it's temporary.

"We should go in." I gesture to the door.

Missa nods and follows me up the brick steps. Ivy twists and twines around the handrails on either side. Green leaves and brown vines almost obscure the small silver doorbell. I reach up a hand and clang the matching silver knocker against the dark green door.

Only a few seconds later, Erin pulls the door open and steps back to let us in. There isn't much of a foyer to speak of. The front door leads to a massive, Victorian-looking sitting room. A hallway straight ahead leads deeper into the house; a set of wooden stairs between the hallway and living room lead up to the second floor; to the left, an archway takes you directly into the large kitchen and dining room.

Already in her outfit for the day, hair done and face made-up, Erin takes one look at me and says, "Coffee?"

I nod and follow her to the kitchen. Missa hangs her coat on the six-pronged standing hanger tucked into the corner by the door and disappears up the stairs.

Erin makes for the counter, her back to me. "How're you doing?"

I squint at her. Something about her tone... is she asking to ask? Or because Missa said something to her?

I decide to give the not-paranoid answer. "Fine. Just tired. We got up early."

She turns from the counter, coffee pot in one hand, mug in the other. An eyebrow raises and she flashes me one of her genuine – like little kid in a candy store genuine – grins. "Coffee."

I nod. "Coffee."

This is why you choose the not-paranoid answer. If I'd gone on the defensive, she'd have known something was wrong.

Which it isn't. Nothing's wrong.

I take the mug from her and sit on one of the wooden barstools along the edge of the kitchen island.

"How are things going over here?"

Erin shrugs, pouring herself a cup and leaning against the granite across from me. "Not much happening at the moment. The girl has a lot of questions. I give her the standard answers, but that's not really ever enough."

"Not for the ones who work out," I agree. "It's good when they want more."

Erin sips from her mug. "She's hungry for it. Angry. She tries to hide it, but she's angry."

I take a moment to respond, sipping from my own mug until my mouth is used to the heat. Then I gulp down the thick, rich, bean-water.

"Wouldn't you be?"

She blows a burst of air out of her mouth. "If I went through half of what the girls you bring me went through…" She shakes her head. "Let's just say I wouldn't have the patience to go through training. I'd be ready to kill someone the minute I knew how."

I raise my mug in a mock salute. She clinks hers against it. "That's why I send 'em here first. You know what to look for."

She nods, straightens, sets her cup on the island, and stretches with a groan. "We haven't eaten yet. You want some food?"

My stomach rumbles. "When have you ever known me to turn down food?"

Erin points an immaculate silver-tipped finger at me as she moves toward the fridge. "I know for a fact you've turned down Missa's kale smoothie about a hundred times."

I stick out my tongue. "Kale isn't food; that doesn't count."

She laughs a low, rumbling, infectious laugh that seems to pour straight from her heart. "I can't argue with that."

She pulls a box of donuts from the fridge and slaps them triumphantly on the counter. Of course, half a dozen containers of fruit are close behind. I inhale a chocolate donut, then fill a bowl with chopped strawberries, apple chunks, sliced bananas, and whole blueberries. I fish out a tiny silver fork from the silverware drawer, and chow down on my bowl of goodness.

Fifteen minutes and a heated conversation about the latest John Wick movie later, Missa and Delilah join us downstairs. I wait for them to grab some grub, refill my coffee, and then we all head into the living room.

I don't like the living room. It's not my style, and I find it to be a bit much. Missa thinks it's hilariously "unique," and Erin obviously likes it or she'd have changed it by now. So I keep my opinion to myself.

From the weird green carpet with golden floral accents, to the antique wooden couches with curved arms, to the light brackets built into the walls, the room looks like an odd step back through time.

A small fire, started by Erin just before we arrived, has burned down to one large, crumbling log. The fireplace is massive. The brick takes up half of the far wall. The wide mantle holds a few old books, some empty glass perfume bottles, a bowl of potpourri, and several large candles.

Erin warms herself by the fire. Delilah settles on the largest of the couches. Missa gazes at a picture on the wall behind the couch, and I sit on the edge of the heavy slice of wood-turned-coffee-table in the center of the room.

Silence fills the big room, broken by the occasional crackle as the flames find a pocket of sap or air in the wood.

I stare down at my coffee, watching the dark liquid circle around and around and around. My mind drifts. Someone clears their throat, and I blink.

I look up. Delilah sits directly ahead of me, gazing intently at my face. The edge of my mouth twitches in a half-grin.

I straighten, stretching my neck and letting out a content groan with my first words. "Well, we usually start with a bit of an explanation about what we do. But I think you probably have a pretty good idea given what happened in Tokyo."

She nods. "Lacey stole information. She said you guys saved people. She stopped…" She clears her throat. "She stopped Mr. Jacobson from killing that reporter. But everyone thought she was a whore."

"Yeah. We save people. But it's more complicated than that. This organization works on three levels." I hold up my fingers. "On the surface, and to the public, I run a publishing company: Miss Belle's Travel Guides. I, with the help of my guides, write travel books about a wide range of places, things to do there, events… that kind of thing. The publishing company angle serves two purposes. To the outside world, we," I gesture at Missa, "give the girls who work for us access to a degree and experience in publishing."

I pause and take a drink of my coffee. The caffeine is finally kicking in. I'm feeling a bit more alive now.

"The next level of the business is one you're already familiar with. In the eyes of most of the high-ranking politicians out there, the big business men, a few members of royalty here and there, and several warlords, we run an escort business. One of the most exclusive on the market. It takes more than money to hire a girl from Miss Belle."

As much as I hate referring to myself in the third person, I do grin as a rush of pride flows through my chest. It took a long time and more than a few disagreements – verbal and physical – for us to build that reputation. Even now, there are still plenty of people who think they can throw more zeros on their offer, and they'll get to own someone for a few days. Daniel Jacobson, for example.

Delilah nods, her brown eyes still fixed on me with a strong level of intensity.

"That leads us to the third level of our organization. What we are, above everything else that everyone thinks we are, is spies." Behind Delilah, Missa sticks out her tongue at me. She finds it both dumb and cliché for us to call ourselves spies.

"Spies," I continue. "Detectives, undercover agents of good, occasionally assassins."

Delilah's eyes widen.

I lift and drop my left shoulder in a half-shrug. "Basically, we work, sometimes individually, sometimes with certain government acronyms, to stop bad people from doing bad things."

"Sometimes the mission-oriented side of the business requires someone to be an escort. You saw that with Lacey in Tokyo," Missa adds. "Our guides are never just escorts. If we send someone on that kind of mission, there is *always* another reason."

I nod. "And joining us, joining our group and doing what we do... that's just the first half of the offer. You don't have any obligation to be a part of," I shake my head, "of any of it. If you want a normal, quiet, calm life, that is your prerogative."

Delilah opens her mouth, confusion on her face.

"That's your right," I elaborate. "You're allowed to choose door number two. We have a fund set aside for women who want out of whatever hell they're a part of with no strings attached. If you want, we can send you to a mid-level college or trade school. We will pay for your room, board, and tuition for the entirety of your education. Then we will finance you for a full year while you build whatever business, career, and life you want for yourself."

"We get you new documentation or freshen up anything you have as long as it's not compromised." Missa's voice glides over us. "We have a list of cities. You can go almost anywhere you want on this Earth. You can be free of your past. You don't have to work with us unless you absolutely want to."

Silence follows her words. Delilah's eyes are still wide like a doe, and I worry we have overwhelmed her.

I sip my coffee, replace the mug with my bowl of fruit sitting on the table next to me, and shovel some strawberries into my mouth. I chew and swallow, then break the silence.

"You don't have to choose now. This house is a waystation. You can take a few more weeks to make your decision."

Her dark hair is already shaking as she moves her head back and forth. "How?" Delilah glances from Missa to me. "How do I do it?

I survey her for a few seconds, then nod.

"She is where you start." I point a finger at Erin, leaned up against the brick fireplace. "Three months here, learning what this life is, seeing if you have the potential to handle it. If Erin says you've got the stuff, you start training for real. A full year just training. Then you'll go on a few soft ball missions." I shake my head. "Plenty of people think the first three months are hard enough, but it gets harder."

She meets my gaze, unwavering with her striking almond-colored eyes.

"Is there a way to do it faster?"

I glance at Missa, leaning her forearms on the back of the couch. She raises her eyebrows, giving me a grin that's holding back a laugh. After a pause, she straightens and comes around the couch to stand by me.

"We can talk about your timetable after the probation period is over. Erin will be evaluating you throughout to see if you have what it takes."

"I do." Delilah gives a sharp, fierce nod.

Erin sighs from her place at the mantle. "That's what they all say." She pushes herself away from the bricks and walks over to us, giving Delilah a hard look. "Do you want to know how many girls get past me?"

My gaze flicks over to Delilah in time to see her swallow. Then her face takes on that same determined look Lacey told me about, and she shakes her head.

"I don't care how anyone else did. I'll make it."

"Good." I stand up. "We'll see you in three months. Until then, Erin will fill us in on your progress."

"I don't see anyone else?" Disappointment lingers in Delilah's voice.

Missa smiles. "You'll be able to see Lacey after your three months. It's important that we can see you take orders from someone else. That you can learn without your hand being held the whole time."

I add, "That you really, truly know you want to do this before we introduce you to anyone else. Protecting our people is the most important part of our job. We don't know you yet."

She seems to think this over for a moment. Her bottom lip disappears between her teeth and she chews on it a few times.

Finally, she tilts her head at me and asks, "What's the second purpose? You said the travel guides have two purposes, to give the girls degrees and?"

I smile. I love it when they catch that. "We use the books to launder money."

Her eyes widen along with my grin.

"A good portion of our finances have to go through a... legitimizing process. Unnamed sources buy massive amounts of travel guides and donate them to schools, libraries, and shelters across the U.S. We get a fat chunk of royalties while only losing maybe 10% of the cash. And our unnamed sources get a nice tax break for their donations."

She nods slowly. Missa catches my eye and gives an approving grin. Not everyone catches that gap in the information. It's a good sign.

We say our goodbyes. Erin promises to call within the week to let us know how things are going. A cab ride later, Missa and I board the plane back to New York. It's almost noon by the time we land, but my day has just started. Next up, a long conversation with a certain police captain.

I call the precinct we live in once we land in New York. Missa drives us through light Saturday afternoon traffic as I schedule a meeting with Captain Wallace. I'd prefer to barge in and demand a lift on the surveillance currently making my life more difficult than it needs to be, but—as Missa puts it—polite diplomacy will probably be a better approach. Polite diplomacy and maybe a fruit basket.

The mildly rude front desk sergeant makes the appointment for Monday at 8 a.m. Yay. I get to wake up early.

My next call is to my little sister, Emily. Damen has been in Brooklyn for over a week now, back undercover as a buyer for an international art collector. It's the best way for me to subtly support my sister without her wondering how a travel writer has the money to help her out.

According to an email I received from him yesterday, Em has a new abstract painting I absolutely have to buy. He (jokingly, I think) threatened to quit if I don't let him hang it on the second-floor corridor next to his bedroom door.

"What's up?" Em's distracted voice says after the fourth ring.

"Hey, just wanted to say hi, see what's new with you."

What sounds like laughter echoes over the phone. I pull it from my ear and hit the speaker button. Missa glances at me, and I shake my head, rolling my eyes.

"Oh, well cool. Nice to hear from you!" There's a scuffling sound followed by a shushing. "Not a lot of new stuff over here, just getting ready for finals."

"I was wondering if you'd be available for lunch sometime this coming week. I haven't been by to see your artwork in a while. Do you have anything new?"

"Uh, yeah. I've got a couple new pieces. We should probably do lunch soon. I've already got a buyer for both of them."

Both of them? Hmm. I wonder if she's talking about Damen. He and I only discussed buying one.

"How does Wednesday work? I've got a thing in the morning, but I can be in Brooklyn around eleven."

"I have a three-hour break between classes starting at noon." She giggles at something. I'm going to assume it's not our conversation.

"That's fine for me. Wanna do Atia's?"

"What? Oh, yeah. Can you text me where you want to meet? I'll see you on Wednesday!"

I manage to squeeze in the word "bye" before she hangs up on me.

"Why does she answer the phone if she doesn't want to talk?" Missa grumbles next to me.

I too am slightly irritated, but I can't get mad. I'm just glad she's laughing. Em has had some troubles in the past. She struggles with depression and anxiety. Whoever was making her laugh like that is good in my book.

I call Damen next to let him know I'll be in Brooklyn on Wednesday. Maybe he and I can meet up after my lunch and discuss when he'll be coming home, what he wants to do for his next mission, and, hopefully, when he'd like to head to Peru for a visit. Based on my last report from the area, things have cooled down. He's been itching to go.

The call goes to voicemail, and Missa gives a firm nod. "That's how you do it. He doesn't want to talk to you—"

I shoot her a glare which she notices from her peripheral vision.

"Or... he's busy. You know what I mean. The point is, he doesn't answer just to end up rushing you off the phone."

"I get your point." I lean my head against the headrest and close my eyes. "But I'm having a lot of trouble actually caring right now."

The temperature in the car drops about five degrees. I peek an eye open and catch Missa staring at me while we idle at a stop light. Her expression is dark: mouth in a tight line, eyebrows drawn together behind the thin frames of her glasses, nostrils twitching with her sharp breaths.

"Caring about this? Or caring in general?"

"What?" I open my other eye and frown at her, puzzled.

"You heard me."

"About this. About people answering the phone just to hurry and end the conversation. What do you mean? 'Caring in general?'"

She shakes her head. "Never mind. I just... I just wanted to check on you after this morning."

I sigh. How many times are we going to need to go through this? "For the last time. It was just a weird moment. Nothing to get hung up on."

"Okay." She nods, but the tone of her response makes me think things are anything but okay.

She doesn't understand. I'm fine. Really, totally, absolutely fine. I just need some time to get back to normal. I just need some time.

"What?" Missa asks.

I muttered those last words. Oops. "I just..." I sigh again. "I just need a little time, Missa. Okay?"

There is a quiet pause, pierced by a car horn somewhere to our left.

"Yeah," she finally responds. "I get it. Some time."

"Good."

I turn my gaze to the city chugging along past the window. My phone, still clutched in my hand, vibrates loudly. I flip it open and read the short text from Damen.

-Busy, sorry. I'll check in later-

After another fifteen minutes, Missa pulls the little Prius into one of the three spaces in the Manor garage. My motorcycle, a beautiful cherry red Ducati, fills another spot. Missa was kind enough to collect it from the airport after the mission in Thailand. And good thing too, the rates for overnight parking are ridiculous. The third space is empty.

Our walk from the garage to the house gives us a mildly impeded view of the street. Between the branches of a flowering hydrangea, I glare at the gray van still parked at the curb across the street.

At this point, I feel like the neighbors have to be noticing it. The magnetic electrician sticker is starting to peel off the side.

"Hope Monday goes well." Missa peeks over my shoulder and shakes her head. "I'm worried."

I raise an eyebrow at her as we climb up the little stone steps leading to the side door.

She elaborates, "They wouldn't be there this long if they didn't have something to go on, right?"

I shrug and push open the door, gesturing for Missa to head into the kitchen first. I follow her, flipping the lock behind me. "Somehow, in our eight years in this business, dealing with the cops like this hasn't really come up. So, I don't know. I hope not. I honestly hope McKinnan is just butthurt about me being a bitch to him."

"He was watching us before that. The gala just pushed him to start parking a van out front."

My chest tightens at this. She's right. He followed me home from the gala, and that was over two weeks ago. They shouldn't have the funding to be running surveillance this long.

I jut my jaw to the side, clicking my teeth in annoyance. Missa hands me a slightly stale snickerdoodle from the cookie-jar replica of the Manor. A gift from Sarah on my twenty-fifth birthday. Definitely one of my top favorite things in this house.

"Have you thought anymore about going to see Doc?" Missa's voice is slightly muffled. Her head is in the fridge.

I pretend not to hear her. I don't want to start a fight, but she won't drop this stupid "go see Doc" thing. By the time I hear the fridge door close, I'm already halfway down the hall.

When I hit the stairs, I do a jog—wincing and holding my ribs—so she won't catch up with me. Her boots click on the hardwood, but I'm at the steps to the third floor and not looking back. I shut my door with a purposeful click, cross to my bed, and sprawl, fully clothed, onto the silk sheets. There's work to do, but my eyes close, my breathing mellows, and I fall asleep with the cookie still clenched in my hand.

Chapter Three

Damen

Long Flights

I don't go straight to the airport. I planned to, but as my taxi careens toward my hotel where a go-bag complete with cash and a passport awaits, we get close to the church I attend while in Brooklyn. A cathedral, really, much like the ones from home I miss with every fiber of my soul.

"Stop up here, please," I choke out.

The driver, a thin man with a pencil mustache and a wrinkled collared shirt, pulls to the curb. I pay him and ask that he stay a few minutes. With a glare and a grumble, he nods.

St. Rose of Lima. A fitting place for me to find God out here, as it holds the name of my home. I found it before Em and I began... whatever it is we have. And, though it is much farther from the Manor than the other handful of Cathedrals in the area, it's still the one I go to for weekly mass. The thirty minute drive is worth it for the name alone.

I hurry inside, pushing through the massive wooden doors. I kneel at the first row of benches and dip my fingers into the holy water, marking a cross before my body.

There are few people here. It's Sunday, but I'm between services. Still, a few older women cluster to the left of the white-turreted altar and the first few rows of benches. The

Father is chatting with a young couple, the woman pressing a hand over her round belly.

He offers me a wave and a nod as I step into the aisle. I take a seat in the middle, under an arching ceiling, stretching into the sky as if the architect wanted the roofers to get personal help from God.

I murmur the Rosary in Spanish. There is no effort, no pulling from my memory as the words spill from my tongue. They come as naturally as breathing.

Then I close my eyes, bow my head, and pray.

Conflict stirs within me. I've trained for this. Trained for this kind of mission, though I've never actually killed anyone. I've assisted. Been there as backup, to help provide a cover, to be the getaway driver. But those were always assigned missions.

And this... this is personal. This is revenge.

I swallow.

How would my father react? He wanted us to be strong. Wanted me and my sisters to have everything he didn't. Everything he couldn't. So much that he worked himself to death to provide, to send us to school.

This wasn't the life he envisioned for me. He thought I'd be a politician or businessman. He died thinking I'd lift our family, lift Peru. He died thinking I'd help people.

But I do.

I shake my head a fraction of an inch as the thought pierces my self-doubt.

I do help people. Miss Belle helps people. The way we do it might not be the most ethical—certainly not to church standards—but we get the job done.

An image of Buccero's new assistant, Arturo, flashes through my mind. The smallest twinge of his shoulder as Buccero touched him. Fury and nausea stir in my stomach.

I open my eyes and look ahead. Jesus hangs from his cross at the front of the church. His eyes are turned upward. A silent plea to God to forgive those who harmed him. My sweaty fists clench at my sides.

I am not Jesus. I am a sinner. We all are, but with my chosen profession, I believe the Father would consider me further gone than the average person.

I can do good. This I know. This I know in my bones the way I feel my faith in my heart. I can stop Buccero from hurting anyone else.

A chill runs down my limbs. My chest fills with warmth. With purpose. I bow my head again, make another sign of the cross, and return to my cab.

Frustration courses through me. My mother would be disappointed in my entitlement. One of the boons of working for Miss Belle is the perfectly planned missions. First class flights, short layovers, the occasional private plane, and a fast track through security most of the time.

None of which I have now, because this mission is entirely off book and without the backing of the guides.

As I fidget in what feels like a mile long security line at JFK, I try to focus on the fact that I'm finally going home – rather than the four-hour long layover I will have to sit through in Panama before I arrive in Lima.

If I'd felt like waiting, I could have left on Monday and gotten a shorter flight. But Buccero's smile is burned into my brain. I see it every time I close my eyes.

He was never supposed to smile like that again.

Security waves me through. I lace up my leather shoes, buckle my belt, and hitch the go-bag over my shoulder.

The wait will give me time for research. The kind of research Missa usually does before every mission. Double checked by Miss Belle. Spelled out in sometimes excruciating detail until we know the plan "front, back, and sideways," as she likes to say.

This time, it's just me. I've watched, helped, but never done the intel gathering like this before.

Never gone off on my own.

Unless you count my time with Emily. Technically my purpose in Brooklyn is always to buy a piece of her art at an exorbitant price and help her get through the next few months of rent. While that still happens, it wouldn't be unfair to say I go off book on those assignments.

I slide into a seat facing the window and briefly watch a plane taxi in while I pull out my tablet.

Booking a few nights in Lima is quick and easy. I have a friend who bartends at a hostel in the center of the city, a good spot for quick movements in an area I've grown unfamiliar with.

How much has my city changed?

In the next two hours before my flight – which ends up delayed – leaves, I find what I need. Enough to get me started, at least. I pinpoint Buccero's new office building in San Isidro, the business district of Lima. I learn he is returning to his villa on the outskirts of the city, in a quiet region away from prying eyes.

My restless fingers pick up my phone more than once, itching to call Emily. To call Miss Belle or Missa or my family.

I text Em instead, a smiley face and a thumbs up in response to her asking how it's going at the airport.

The others though... this isn't their fight. I don't know what Miss Belle would say about my plan. I can't risk her trying to talk me out of it. Or worse, ordering me back home and keeping me somewhere safe while she handles it herself.

I wonder what that would look like. If Buccero would end up in prison again. Or if Miss Belle would be the one behind bars this time.

The thought sends a shudder down my spine. What would the Guides become without her?

Better not to risk it. Better to handle it myself.

I click off my phone, the image of my sisters and mother fading to a black screen as the speaker overhead announces boarding has started.

I sleep on the first leg of the flight and have enough nightmares that the second is spent in brutal anxiety.

A pungent bag of onion chips in the row behind me makes my stomach churn. An argument several seats ahead sends sharp pains across my temples.

I play with the chain around my neck as the plane hits a bit of turbulence. The sounds and smells around me fade into the background as I focus on the texture of the metal against my skin.

I was fifteen when my father died. He worked himself into an early grave to give my sisters and me a better life. We had enough money for my twin, Carmen, to get through college. But I wanted to work a few years first – save up enough for me and our little sister Rosie too.

Buccero hired me when I was eighteen. Fresh out of high school and not at all qualified to be the executive assistant of an advisor to the President and the CEO of a major corporation.

The plan was to work for a year and then join my sister at school. After the first year was up, I wasn't allowed to leave. He wanted me close.

Ambition put me by his side.

Fear kept me there.

The white-hot anger tensing my shoulders is doing a good job of burning out my fear. I can be honest with myself, if not with anyone else, and say that I am terrified of my plan. I am terrified of what will happen if I fail.

But things are different now. I spent a year training when I left Peru. The next two were plentiful with missions and assignments that tested every aspect of me. Physical capability. Mental strength. Wit and brains and cunning and so much more.

When the plane touches down in Lima, Peru, the fear has diminished to a low murmur in the back of my mind. I shoot a text to Em, a mere pittance of my promise to stay in touch, and let her know I landed safely.

The sky outside is dark, the local time nearly midnight. I grip the cross around my neck as tires hit the tarmac. Without needing to wait for checked luggage, I sling my go-bag over my shoulder and step outside.

Air is air. Some places have a thinner atmosphere, some have more pollution, some have different smells. But air is air.

Even still, as I step through the sliding glass doors and breathe in Lima, tears fill my eyes. Home. The ground beneath my feet cradles me. The air caresses my bare arms. Even the stars above me, though I can't actually see them, are the way they are supposed to be now.

I breathe for a few long seconds, then I hail a taxi.

The man driving has a full mustache and wears a faded and worn Chicago Bulls baseball cap. His skin is dark, his smile not meeting his eyes as he speaks to me in broken English.

I glance at my reflection in the back window as he tells me how much a drive into the Lima district (a central district in the city that shares its name) will cost. Have I gotten that pale? Do I look so much like an American that I can pass for a tourist?

It must be so, because the price he gives me is about double what it should cost. I laugh, the sound hollow as that white strike of fury sparks again. When I lean down to meet his gaze through the open passenger window, I bare my teeth.

"I must have lost color during my time away for you to take me for some kind of tourist," I say in Spanish, my accent singing through every word. "I'll pay half what you ask."

There is a brief pause, then the man cracks into a genuine smile and agrees.

I climb in.

I should be on my phone, messaging my contacts and preparing to pick up the supplies I couldn't fly with, but I can't tear my eyes from the window.

Lima whirls by. Buildings tower above me; cars swerve close, ignoring the faded lines painted on the asphalt, nearly skimming the red paint on this tiny car. Packed buses, full of people heading home from a long day of labor. Patches of green grass, parks and museums and cafes. Late night pedestrians, walking dogs, going home from work, moving through their city – my city – in such a natural way.

Nostalgia burns like coals in the pit of my stomach, aching and bringing tears to my eyes. There is sadness in it. Sadness to accompany the relief when I find that I can map each turn the driver takes. The streets have remained familiar, even three years later.

We pull to the side of the road just in front of the Museo de Arte, a place filled with such beauty that I could spend hours walking its halls. I want to bring Em here. To show her the kind of galleries her art deserves to be in.

That can't happen until Buccero is gone.

I step out of the cab and fetch my go-bag from the trunk. It's lucky I bring one every time I go to Brooklyn. It has everything I need for a venture like this—except the weapons. I didn't even need to go back to the manor for my passport. A good thing, as I'd probably have lost my nerve for this plan if I had to tell anyone about it.

Across the street from the museum is a tall, clean building with a secured and bolted front door. I push the little button on the side and give a wave to the camera above it.

There is a grinding sound and the door pops open. I close it firmly behind me, trek up the stairs, and lean against the dark wood of the L-shaped front desk.

1900 Backpacker's Hostel is one of the nicer places to stay for people who are broke, adventurous, or friendly. Mustard-colored, wide marble stairs lead up to the front desk and an open, living room type area. Couches, chairs, and desks form two semi-circles. Two public computers, a good five years out of date, are accessible via the dollar coins we use in Peru. A sign on the wall announces the WiFi information. One of the computers is taken by an ambiguous figure with long blonde hair. The screen lights up their silhouette. They're checking their Instagram feed.

The ceilings are high, the rooms are spacious, cheap, and clean, and the bar has a pool table. One could ask for nothing more.

"*Hola.*" I grin down at the petite girl behind the check-in desk. She's hunched over a textbook in front of the monitor. Cameras, two showing different angles of the front door, two in the bar, and one in the courtyard, wink up from the screen.

"Do you have a reservation?" She doesn't look up from her book.

"Yes, under Damen."

She flips open a large booklet on the adjoining section of the desk. "A private room?" Her gaze still has not left the textbook.

"Yes." I'm grinning. This sort of customer service isn't heard of in the U.S. or the fancier, touristy hotels. Yelp users would slaughter this girl. I am vaguely entertained.

"I need to make a copy of your passport, I need a credit card, and how many days you're staying. The price will be thirty sols a night."

I fish out my wallet, place my passport and card on the desk, and say, "I paid for two nights online."

She finally looks up at me, her thin eyebrows drawn together in an irritated frown. "Keep the card then." She looks at my bag: not a backpacker's pack, not a tourist's suitcase. Then she gives me a once over, taking in the expensive clothes I probably should have toned down. They're wrinkled from the flight, but still higher quality than she's used to.

Her frown deepens. She takes the passport from the counter—a fake, but the best money can buy—and scans it through a copier.

I flash a smile. "I know someone who used to work here, maybe still does. Gabriel?"

The frown converts into incredulously raised eyebrows and a sideways smile. "You are friends with Gabriel?"

"Yes. Since primary school."

She squints her eyes at me, picks up a cell phone which had been hidden under the textbook, and types rapidly, her long dark nails clicking on the screen.

She sets the phone face down on the book and stands up. The movement from seated to standing positions doesn't make much of a difference in her height. I'm short, but I have whole inches over this girl.

"We have rules. You have to check out by 11 a.m. Be respectfully quiet in the sitting area, but the bar is pretty open. Free breakfast in the morning will be in the bar. Coffee, juice, bread, and jam. If you don't like it," she gives me a look daring me to not like it, "there are plenty of restaurants a few blocks up the street."

I nod. "Thanks."

She takes me down a long, dark, corridor. She points out the men's room. We make two lefts and a right, and she unlocks a large white door. "This is your room. This is your key." She hands it to me. "Don't lose the key."

I nod again.

"If you want, I'll show you the bar."

"That would be great." I toss my bag onto one of the three beds, a single and a bunk bed, and lock the door behind me.

We've taken three steps when a voice shouts from the darkness in front of us.

"No fucking way!"

I recognize that voice. It would be impossible for me not to.

Gabriel steps into the light. He's a little heavier, a lot hairier, and his natural exuberance is just as I remember. "What the hell are you doing here?"

The smile spreading across my face is impossible to contain. "Gabe!" I step forward to meet him, and he throws his arms around me in a tight hug.

We separate, and he slaps a hand on my shoulder. "Why didn't you tell me you were coming? I've gotta work all week. I could have asked for some time off. I haven't seen you in forever."

The front desk girl clears her throat. "I'm gonna go. You two enjoy," she waves her hand in a little circle, "whatever this is."

Her sandals clip clop against her feet as she marches away.

Gabe rolls his eyes. "She's a gem, really. My favorite of the new hires."

I laugh. "Sorry I didn't call, my friend. My trip was pretty last minute. I'm just passing through Lima."

Gabe nods and gestures for me to follow him. "I've got to get back to the bar before the Australians get too crazy. Come hang out while I work."

The bar is crowded. Sure enough, four Aussies clamor for Gabe to grab them more beers as soon as he steps through the door. A couple of Nigerians play table soccer, shouting with glee at every score, and a pair of very old looking French men smoke thick cigars on the balcony.

Gabe gestures to a stool, and I sit. He circles the counter, grabs the Aussies their beers, and gives me a questioning look.

"Wine, red, whatever you've got."

With a nod, he turns his back, fills a glass, and faces me again. "So, what are you doing here?"

I sip the wine. It's not as fruity as I prefer. "I have some business to take care of."

Gabe watches me for a moment, curiosity in his gaze. "Is it an impromptu trip? Are you visiting family at all?"

I lean back, my gaze hardening as I look at my old friend. "Why do you ask?"

"I talked to Carmen yesterday; she didn't say anything about you coming to visit." He pulls a rag from beneath the bar and begins the process of wiping down sticky spots.

"I didn't know you and Carmen were talking." My voice comes out flat. More deadpan than I mean it to.

Gabe flushes. "She called me up for a favor a couple weeks ago. It's been long enough, Damen. I got over my issues."

I grasp my cross, my other hand delicately twirling the stem of my wine glass. Anxiety churns in my stomach. My family isn't supposed to be contacting people from our past.

Neither am I.

"How are you doing?" I ask, taking a sip of my drink.

Gabe's eyes widen a fraction, startled by the sudden shift in conversation. I've got too much anxiety in my gut to chat about my family right now.

He tells me about his life. The things I missed these last three years. The stuff we missed before that, after my sister dumped him, and I got a job in Lima, and we stopped hanging out together.

There was a time the three of us were inseparable. But this is the first time I've spoken to him in almost five years.

It feels like nothing has changed as we dive into his life. His relationships, his degree in photography, how much he loves working at a hostel and meeting people from all over the world. I sidestep equally genuine and curious questions, letting him fill the conversation while I listen. When he questions my silence, I wave away concerns with a response about jet lag.

"I have to run an errand tomorrow," I say as the hour slips past one in the morning. Most of the bar has filtered out and gone off to bed or whatever adventure awaited them next.

Gabe nods. "We close down in a bit anyway. Want to grab a bite tomorrow?"

"Plan on Tuesday?" I ask. "I'll be out of the city most of the day tomorrow. But we can grab breakfast Tuesday morning before I leave."

Gabe's face falls. "I was hoping you'd be staying longer than a couple days."

I slide my glass across the bar toward him. "I'll be back. If this trip goes the way I plan, I'll be back often."

Gabe raises an eyebrow but says nothing else except goodnight. We share another hug. I trudge to my room, find my pillow, and slip into a fretful sleep.

Airports are odd. They are liminal spaces where time has little meaning, food is either overabundant or nonexistent, and the art is often very Alice-in-Wonderlandy. Take JFK for example; the giant apple is great. A fun nod to NYC, a colorful art installation, and a great photo op. But also, it's a giant apple in an airport. Weird.

As someone who travels often, people-watching is just another surreal piece of art when flying. Not all countries view security the same way, which leads to a veritable cornucopia of confusion when traveling internationally.

Folks from the good ol' U.S. of A, most places don't need you to take off your shoes... heck, they don't want you to. And, for our lovely friends from across the various seas, don't be too startled when Americans get undressed to a weird comfort level when they're going through security.

It's pretty simple as long as you follow the signs, do what you're told, and don't wear bedazzled pants (you will get *pulled to the side for a pat-down when the metal detector glitches out).*

CHAPTER FOUR
DAMEN
OLD LADIES WITH GUNS

Finding a rental car is easy enough. Driving north, past Lima's city limits and up the coast, is a simple task. Remembering where Miss Belle's Peruvian contact is without calling her for directions is another story.

I cross off a series of towns and villages on my way up the coast. There are images in my head from the single time Miss Belle brought me to Señora Luccela's, but beyond recognizing a few distinct features, I don't have a real plan for finding her.

I could always try calling home. I wouldn't necessarily even have to talk to Miss Belle. I roll my eyes as I pass a turn off to a cliff-side overlook. Speaking to anyone at the manor would get word back to my boss. We're a loyal bunch.

The countryside distracts me from my stress for a while. The road dips and swerves to the edge of the seaside cliffs and further inland as I breathe in the salty air and take in the beauty around me. On my other side, lush forest extends as far as I can see. My eyes are fixed on my surroundings, searching.

An hour later I consider giving up. I know how hard it will be to find weapons by myself, but the bubbling frustration in my gut promises I can make it happen.

A blue sign slips past. I blink and hit the brakes. Put the little rental in reverse and backtrack. There. A pale blue sign with faded black lettering.

I've found the town. Step one: complete.

I pull off at the correct exit and roll slowly down the streets. It's late afternoon at this point. Thanks to my flight, three glasses of wine, and reconnecting with Gabe, it was a slow morning.

The town is small. I drive past a restaurant, the expansive outdoor seating area full of tourists munching lunch before they continue their coastal travels. There's a little hotel with a broken window but a cute sign announcing open rooms. It all looks vaguely familiar, but nothing sparks a true memory until I pass the market.

I hook a left onto a gravely dirt road and bump along for over a mile. It's slow going. Eventually, a massive, gnarled and twisted blackened tree comes into view. I make a right, follow a dusty drive, and park in front of an old but well maintained cottage. There's another car in the drive, a beat-up yellow Volkswagen Bug.

I recognize everything except the car.

A light drizzle starts up as I step from my rental and walk to the front door. The house is a faded russet brown. A black door, black framed windows, and black trim give the whole thing a slightly spooky demeanor.

I wish I could take a picture to send to Em. She'd love to paint a house like this, with the metal cylinder chimney, the rickety porch, and the small shed out back.

But having something like that on my phone would be stupid beyond reason. Maybe I can describe it to her when I get back.

My gaze lingers on the wooden building before I climb the porch steps. I knock.

There is a slight commotion inside, a few muffled words exchanged between two people, and finally the door opens.

"Uh." I frown at the man before me before sliding a smile onto my face. "*Hola*, I'm here to see Señora Luccela."

"*Claro*." A polite, yet stiff, smile replaces the firm line that had been the man's expression. He's as dark as the Señora. Smooth charcoal skin and tight, curly hair. He's my age, maybe a little older, and regards me with suspicious eyes. "*Abuela* is inside. Please, come in."

He gestures forward, and I step through the doorway, a prickle going up the back of my neck. When I was here with Miss Belle three years ago, we'd only met with Señora Luccela. I don't know how much this stranger is allowed to hear.

The inside is comfortably musty. The scent of cinnamon and moth balls fills the small home. The señora sits in a padded rocking chair in the corner of the living room, a pair of knitting needles clicking together with each back and forth of the rocker.

"Have a seat," the man says.

I cross to the couch, uncomfortable with my back to the kitchen and the door I catch a glimpse of while moving through the room. My unease settles a bit as the man sits on a wooden chair on the other side of the fireplace.

Señora Luccela barely looks up as I enter, but once I perch on the edge of the couch, she sets her knitting to the side and examines me. Her hair is as stark white as I remember, vibrant against her dark skin. Wide brown eyes are magnified by the insect-like glasses she wears. A crochet shawl wraps around her frail shoulders, and a blanket rests on her lap, its fringed edges touching the floor.

"I remember you," she croaks out.

I lick my lips and suck in a deep breath. "Yes, thank you for having me again, Señora. I was here a few years ago with my employer..." I glance at the man.

Señora Luccela waves a wrinkled hand. "Don't worry about my grandson. He knows nothing of the business."

Her words make me more worried. My hand fidgets with the buttons on my shirt.

"What?" Luccela's grandson frowns. "What business?"

She waves a hand again. "Never you mind, Caleb." She leans in, stopping the rocker as she stares at me. "He's here to help me around the house a bit. Apparently, I don't do a good enough job cleaning anymore."

Caleb clears his throat and leans on his knees. He runs a hand across his forehead. "I'm here to help out and make sure you take your meds." He looks at me. "How do you know my *Abuela*?"

"I, uh..." I clear my throat. "Señora Luccela and my employer have a working relationship."

He raises an eyebrow. "What does that mean?"

"Oh hush, Caleb," Luccela snaps. "How is Miss Belle doing?" She smiles warmly at me.

My eyes widen a fraction. "She is well."

"I didn't get any call about an upcoming mission."

Caleb puts up a hand. "Pardon my *Abuela*, she doesn't have a phone."

"*Niño*, don't make me get my spoon," Luccela growls. She sticks her hand between the cushions of the rocking chair and pulls out an old, sturdy model cell phone.

Caleb gapes. "How long have you had that? I've been putting in calls to the doctor for you."

"This is for work, Caleb." Luccela rolls her eyes, the effect hilarious and terrifying with her thick glasses. She looks at me. "As I said, I didn't get a call from Miss Belle. Is there something I should know?"

I clear my throat and smooth my features. "Not at all. She's quite busy at the moment and out of cell range."

Luccela raises an eyebrow as white as her hair, the look so identical to her grandson's I have to stifle a smirk. "I usually hear from her or Missa before someone shows up at my door."

My hand twitches toward my cross, but I tuck it under my thigh instead. "They knew you'd remember me from three years ago. Since we already know each other, they didn't believe calling ahead would be necessary."

"Well." Luccela humphs and gingerly rises from her chair. "I'd have liked to get Caleb out of the house before you showed up."

"What?" her grandson says, affronted.

"Hush and help me, Caleb."

With a low grumble, Caleb crosses to take his *Abuela's* arm. She leans on him. They walk down the narrow hallway leading to the back of the house. I watch for a moment before she calls back, "Are you coming, or not?"

I puff out a breath, my heartbeat slamming as I sort out whether to be amused or concerned. Then I stand, pull the crucifix out from under my shirt, and follow them.

The back door leads to a set of stone steps. Those, in turn, trace a path to the small shed behind the house. I trail behind as Señora Luccela hobbles along, clinging to her grandson and muttering to herself.

The door is padlocked. The señora pulls a ragged square of leather off of two separate keypads beside the handle. She leans close and types into the first one. A green light flickers into place. As she leans into the second, Caleb bends down as well.

Luccela slaps his arm. "No being nosy."

I stifle a chuckle. It's going to be impossible for him not to be nosy after this.

Another green light pops up, there's a beep, and the sound of sliding metal bolts.

Luccela steps to the side and gestures to the door. I glance at Caleb, who raises his hands in a shrug. I move up, grip the handle, and pull.

The door sticks as though it hasn't been opened in quite some time. I heave, and it jerks open.

The interior is dingy. No light, save the beams coming through the open door. The space is small, maybe ten feet by ten feet. A stack of wooden crates sits against the back wall; assorted gardening equipment dangles from hooks on the side.

Caleb sticks his head in. "What is going on, *Abuela*?" he asks, his tone bemused and tired.

"Get that light, will you?" Luccela says. She pokes my upper arm with a bony finger. When I glance over, she cracks a wicked grin.

"Sure," Caleb mumbles.

I look at the ceiling as he goes for the light switch barely visible a few feet in from the door. There are no lightbulbs.

He flicks the switch.

His yelp nearly drowns out the thwap as a wire goes taut over our heads. It's almost invisible, thin as a fishing line, and tied to a trap door hidden by the dirt and dust.

Not so hidden when it slams open, the top cracking into the side of the shed.

Caleb gapes, gaze darting from the hole in the ground on the far side of the shed, to his *Abuela* cackling beside me.

She nudges me with her elbow. "I had that installed a year ago. It gets so hard to bend over in my old age."

I nod, my heart still racing from the slam. I didn't jump like Caleb did, but that little surprise startled me as well.

"All right, well, youth before beauty," she says.

Caleb, breathing heavily and looking like his whole life has been flipped upside-down, shakes his head with a bewildered expression.

I take pity and step forward. The trapdoor covered a hole. About three feet by three feet, nestled against the corner of the shed, and pitch black. The only thing I can see staring down danto it is the faint outline of the first few steps of steep concrete stairs.

"The light is halfway down, on the left," Luccela calls after me.

I plant a foot on the first step and glance back. The last time I was here, Miss Belle and Señora Luccela left me inside the house with a cup of tea and an order not to touch anything.

I swallow.

"Is it actually a light this time?" Caleb grumbles under his breath behind me.

Luccela cackles again.

I put a hand on the wall to my left as I descend—more concrete, cold against my palm—the other gripping my cross. My eyes struggle to adjust to the black. My head goes past the edge of wood above and, just as I contemplate returning to the shed, my fingers hit a bit of plastic. I find the switch, flick it on, and lose the air from my lungs.

Along two of the stark white walls, rows of hooks, shelves, and platforms hold what must be nearly fifty guns. I gape at the array of sizes, uses, cartons of ammunition, and shiny metal plating.

My feet thud limply on the remaining stairs, and I step into the brightly lit space. I circle in the middle of the room, taking it all in. The floor is marble, smooth and white as the walls with waving strips of gray throughout. Cabinets run along the ground on each wall, their doors, handles, and hinges all stark white. They rise nearly to my chest, forming a shelf that rings around the room. Above them is the weapon display across two walls. A third holds a massive map of the world, in proper proportions, marked with red dots. The final wall is hung with vests, bracers, and an assortment of body-pads. The shelf below is lined with heavy-duty tactical boots in an array of sizes.

The place looks like an assassin's wet dream.

How many of Miss Belle's people have gotten to see this? I know her contact in Paris doesn't have a set-up like this. If it did, Alex would spend less time shopping and more time caressing heavy duty semi-automatics.

"*Abuela...*" Caleb's strained voice breaks me out of the reverie.

He's at the bottom of the stairs, gazing around with wide, terrified eyes. Behind him, Señora Luccela hobbles down as well.

She gives a little push on his shoulder to get through then moves straight toward the wall of armor.

"What sort of mission are we dealing with, *niño*? Are you planning on getting shot at?"

My smile widens. It's no surprise Miss Belle likes working with this woman, she's what I imagine my boss will be like when she's that old. Assuming any of us stay alive that long.

"I plan on doing the shooting, but I'll take a vest anyway."

She nods, looks me up and down, then pulls a vest about my size from the wall.

"*Abuela,*" Caleb moans. "What is going on? Who is this? What is *this*?" He gestures around the small room.

"This is how I sent your mother and tias to school on a chicken farmer's salary," she says, barely glancing at him. "You said you wanted to help your *Abuela*, so help." She points to a cabinet. "There are bags in there." Glances at me. "How big do you need?"

I've crossed to a smaller handgun on the wall, a Sig Sauer P365, and pulled it down, examining and admiring the craftsmanship. "Medium."

She nods. "Get a bag from the middle shelf, find out what our client wants to take, and help get things packed up."

Caleb gapes for a brief second, then something clicks in his gaze. He pulls a bag from the cabinet and looks at me. He swallows. "Well?"

I stifle a chuckle and start shopping.

Chapter Five
Miss Belle
Conversations with Cops

I take my motorcycle.

I flex my gloved fingers over the grip on my handlebar. I understand why Lacey did what she did—taking Delilah to a safe-house rather than leaving her to whatever fate awaited her at the hands of her pimp. But still, I didn't have time for the intensive background I usually do before giving new girls the "you have two choices" bit.

I roll my neck at a stoplight. Everything is still tight, still tense, still a fucking mess. My jaw clenches.

Focus. I need to keep focus. Having constant police surveillance isn't good for business.

I pull into the lot, politely waiting for two squad cars to pass, and park my bike right out front. I take off my helmet and run a hand through my auburn hair. Missa blew it out this morning. Bruised ribs—not cracked like I originally thought, thank goodness—limit the amount of time I can actually keep my hands over my head.

I lean down, checking my reflection in the little side mirror. The hair looks pretty good, even with the smushing from a full helmet. My forehead is just about healed, but the flesh is still a little pink where the scar tissue is finishing forming. A bullet graze will do that to you. It's lucky no one can see my back. The slice that separated a flap of skin from my shoulder blade ended up needing stitches. The flesh is still bruised and bloody looking, though I can finally stretch without worrying about everything pulling apart.

My left leg swings over the leather seat, my boot landing firmly on the concrete. A pair of patrol uniforms walk by; a bald meth-addict-looking rail thin guy stumbles between them, hands cuffed behind his back.

I follow them through the glass paneled front doors.

The building bustles. Uniformed officers are grabbing coffee, walking around, talking, doing everything, it seems, except sitting. The plainclothes fellas, all significantly older-looking, are doing the exact opposite. I even spot one taking a nap. To my right, a receptionist-type desk but with a thick plastic casing like at those 24-hour liquor stores seats a disgruntled-looking brunette man. Bags line the underside of his eyes; the lids are half-closed even as he hands the men before me a stack of processing papers.

I offer a bright smile when I step up to the opening. He does not return it.

"Hi," I say, using the voice I generally reserve for an extremely hungover Levi. "I have an appointment with Captain Wallace."

"Up the stairs, take a right, should be the second door down."

"Should be?"

He squints at me, a sneer on his face. "It'll have the name on the door."

I tilt my head and smile that "Well, fuck you, then" smile that I used to use when I worked retail. I pick my helmet up off the bench, bypass a 200lb (most of it in the bust and ass) hooker, and skip up the stairs. My fingers dance along the railing until they hit something sticky, then I firmly stuff my hand into my jacket pocket.

The guy was a little off. I find the black letters that say Capt. Wallace on the third door down the left side. I knock, wait for the "come in," and push open the door.

Captain Suzanne Wallace is a 45-year-old Army veteran with long black hair tightly braided and curled into a bun on the back of her head. Her skin has that weathered, dark leather look, her eyes are alert and intelligent, and she stands a good four inches shorter than me.

When I walk in the room, she steps out from behind her desk and offers me her hand. I shake it politely, then take the seat she gestures to.

"What can I help you with today, Belle?"

"Suzie, how are you? How's Josh and the kids?"

"Kids have the flu. Josh left for L.A. three days ago and will be gone until next week."

I wince and shake my head. "That sucks. Sorry to hear it."

"Ehh, could be worse. My mom retired last year. At least I've got someone at the house to watch them."

I nod. Okay, that's enough of the small talk. I know Suzie from the NYPD annual policeman's balls (haha), and from a few different community participation events. But that's about it. As nice as it is to have a couple cop friends, I'm not out getting lunch with her on a weekly basis or anything.

"So—" I begin.

"I can't do anything about McKinley."

My mouth is still open. I close it. My eyebrows come together as my mouth twists sideways in a frown.

"What do you mean? You're his Captain."

"I'm new. As you know."

"Yeah, the guy at the front desk couldn't even give directions to your office."

She rolls her eyes. "He's just a dick. What I mean is I'm new to being a captain. It took a long time to get this position, I'm not ready to start making waves."

I let out a barely restrained grunt. "You can't just order him to knock it off? He has no right to be parked outside my house all day and night."

"Actually..." She moves around some papers on her desk, picks one out of a blue folder, and hands it to me. "He does. This stays between us, but he got the warrant about two weeks ago. McKinley's been on the job for a long time."

"So, he's got friends in the DA's office."

"Basically."

"Basically? Shit Suzie, that means the DA is looking into me? Why? I'm a goddamn travel writer."

She shakes her head. "I'm not the one who got him a warrant. And I'm not the one who asked him to take the case in the first place."

"'Take the case!' What the hell does that mean? There's a case?" I heave a sigh and rub my hand across my forehead. Pain flashes in the back of my eyes as my hand brushes across the tender new skin above my left eyebrow. I wince again.

"I'm sorry, Belle. It definitely wasn't my idea to have you investigated. I think it's a waste of time." She tilts her head. "And money."

"You're damn right it is." Blood heats up in my chest. This conversation isn't going the way I had planned. I take a couple slow, deep breaths to try and calm myself. Flying off the handle at Suzie isn't the right move. Not yet anyway.

"Isn't there anything you can do? It's just..." I grit my teeth. "It's really annoying having that ass sitting out front every time I leave for the gym."

"I'll do what I can, Belle. But it's pretty high above my paygrade." She grimaces across the desk at me. "I probably shouldn't have said that."

I open my mouth, but she holds up a hand.

"And I can't say anything else about it."

She stands up, and I follow suit.

"Well, thanks for your time, at least," I grumble, somewhat ungratefully. I put the paper—proof of McKinley's legitimate warrant—back on the desk.

"I wish I could do more to help. You're one of our best donors, I haven't forgotten."

I nod and stick out my hand. She shakes it.

"Good luck with the kids."

"Thanks."

Walking with decidedly less spring in my step, I head back down the stairs and out to my motorcycle.

Absolutely *not* buying tickets to the policeman's ball this year.

The ride home is quick. The van is still parked across from the Manor, but I'm not tempted to go confront Detective McKinley this time. Not now that I know his operation is much bigger than I thought.

My foot hits the second stone step leading to the porch when the ornate wooden door opens. Missa looks out at me, a question on her face.

"No luck," I say, pulling off my black leather jacket and hanging it in the hall closet.

Missa glances out the door before pulling it closed. "He's still there."

"Yeah, that would be what 'no luck' meant. Wallace can't do anything about it. And apparently, it's a lot worse than we thought. The DA has a case. McKinley has a warrant. We need to get started on damage control, fast."

"We need to do damage control on a few things."

I stop walking and look at her. "What does that mean?"

"You need to talk to someone about what happened."

My mouth goes dry. I've successfully avoided this conversation since Saturday when I pretended not to hear her. "I thought we were done with this."

She gives me an infuriatingly calm stare. "No. We've barely discussed it."

My front teeth click together at the same time my eyes half-close and a sigh hisses out of my mouth.

"We discussed it enough." I turn away. I point-blank refuse to have this conversation.

"Ana." The sharpness of her voice and the use of my old nickname make me stop.

My chest pounds. A strange heat rushes through my veins. All at once, I'm furious. Anger clouds my eyes; Missa's face blurs in my vision.

"I did what needed to be done!" My voice is louder than I planned. I've shouted at her. I'm standing a foot from her, fists clenched, heart beating fast.

Her blue eyes lock onto mine, and she doesn't blink.

Someone clatters down the stairs. "Is everything..." Josie's voice trails away, and I hear her scurry back up.

Missa watches me still. I feel frozen, locked, trapped. My eyes burn, and my nose itches. I blink first.

"I did what I had to do, Missa."

She reaches out and takes my hand. It's only when her steady fingers wrap around mine that I realize I'm shaking.

"You make all the Guides talk to someone. Why are you exempt from getting help?"

I can't respond. My reply sticks in my throat. So, I take a step and wrap my arms around her. I bury my face in her shoulder, and she holds me for a long moment. The anger drains away as quickly as it appeared.

"You need to talk to Doc, Ana," she mutters in my ear.

"When things slow down." My voice is flat. I have no intention of talking to Doc. And honestly, I have no idea why not. Maybe if I had a concrete reason, I could give it to Missa and she'd drop it. But I don't.

She nods and breaks away from me. "Emily called a while ago to confirm lunch. One of her afternoon classes got canceled so she'll have a few hours of free time."

"That works out," I say, turning away from her and wiping a tear away. "I wanted to hang out."

"And to give her shit for giving your parents your cell number."

"Yeah. That too."

I grab a snack from the kitchen and head upstairs to get changed. Today I'm scheduled for my first workout since I got back from Thailand a week ago. It'll be hard, but Dee will know just how far to push me without giving my body more damage than it already has.

I take the family Prius, a clean change of clothes in my bag on the front seat ready for when I get done.

The rest of the morning burns away in a flurry of light weightlifting, speed-walking— "Absolutely no running for another week, at least"— and exactly one attempted crunch, followed by a moan of pain and several minutes of laying on the floor.

"That must have been quite the climbing trip," Dee says in a wry tone.

I glance over from my place in front of a mirrored wall, grunting as I finish a rep of bicep curls with 10lb weights. "Yep," I huff. "Falling off a mountain sucks."

She nods, coming to stand behind me so we can see each other in the mirror. "I'm impressed you walked away with only bruised ribs."

"And the slice in my back."

"Right…"

I drop my arm without form and stare at her in the mirror. "What's that mean?"

She shrugs and walks away to place a third check-mark next to the workout on the white-board. "Just that I've never seen someone walk away from a fall like you described without getting scraped up all over their body. Your ribs look like you got kicked, not like you fell."

I grind my teeth. My breathing picks up, and I clench the grips of the weights. "It was definitely an interesting trip. I'm not going mountain climbing for a while, I can tell you that."

She runs a tongue over her teeth, her bottom jaw jutting out. An immaculate black eyebrow slides up her forehead as she stares at me. I catch her gaze and hold it, refusing to blink. A moment passes.

She shakes her head and walks away.

I let out a sigh. As much as I love and trust Dee, she's not on the list of people who know what we do. And she won't be. Her job is to get us fit and ready to fight, not to go asking about my injuries.

A small part of my brain understands she is just showing concern for my well being, but I don't need concern. Not from her or Missa.

I give my body a little shake, wincing at the pain in my chest and back, before returning to my reps. Two more before I switch to squats.

A welcome surprise awaits me at the Manor. Or—rather—doesn't await me. The police surveillance van is gone. First time since I've gotten home from Thailand that it hasn't given me a flash of anger as I pull into the garage.

Still, the lack of police presence and a successful—if nosy—workout have put me in an excellent mood. There's a spring in my step as I head to the house.

"Darling!" I sing to Missa as I burst through the kitchen door.

She glances at me from her place at the sink. What looks suspiciously like kale is getting rinsed in a plastic colander. "Someone's in a good mood."

"How could I not be?" A wildly enthusiastic grin takes over my face. "The coppers are gone!"

Josie's head pokes in from the living room. Her tiny hands, fingernails painted the same shade of pink as her hair, clutch an Xbox360 remote. "What's up?"

"The police, my dear." I waltz over to her and plant a kiss on her forehead.

She and Missa raise eyebrows at me. Sarah, sitting in the living room just at the edge of my sight, cackles as she shoots Josie's Halo character.

Josie curses and runs back to her seat.

Missa dries her hands, eyebrow still raised.

"What's happening now?"

"The police are gone." I go to boost myself onto the counter—pain, sharp pain—change my mind, and settle myself at one of the wooden chairs. "That stupid fucking van has finally driven away." I wave my hand in a somber "goodbye" gesture. "We should send Captain Wallace a fruit basket. With muffins. A muffin and fruit basket."

"You sure?"

"Yes. Muffins and fruit are a fantastic way of saying 'thank you.'"

She sighs, a soft smile replacing the quizzical look she's been sporting. "I mean about the police. Are you sure McKinley is gone?"

I lean forward, mildly irritated at her lack of excitement. "It's a big van. It's easy to spot."

"I meant... are you sure they haven't just switched to something a little less obvious?"

I shake my head, unwanted doubts popping into my brain. "Quit ruining my fun."

She laughs. "I'm happy the van is gone. And a fruit basket is a great idea." She raises her voice. "Sarah, Josie, can you two get online and order a nice fruit and muffin basket for our dear friend Captain Wallace?"

There's a scuffle, gunshots on a TV screen, and more cursing.

Sarah's head pokes around the corner, a victorious smile lighting up her face. "Sure. Any particular theme?"

I squint at her, confused. "The theme is fruit and muffins."

Missa chuckles—I glower at her—and shakes her head at Sarah. "It's a thank you basket."

Sarah nods and disappears.

"Right." Missa turns back to the sink, shakes the colander, and dumps a stack of foul leaves onto a big green kitchen towel laid out on the counter. "Back to the matter of the van. I'm glad it's gone and all, but we should be on the lookout for anything strange. They could just be gearing up for something... I don't know... worse?"

My gaze is distant. Like those moments you stare without actually staring and then someone gives you a funny look because you were spacing out in their direction. Missa glances at me, sees my "thinking face" and goes back to making her salad or smoothie or whatever the fuck she's doing with the ugly middle-child of spinach and lettuce.

McKinley is close to getting a warrant for the Manor. Does Wallace have more influence than she thought? Was she able to get the van pulled until McKinley has something more substantial to go on? No—that doesn't make sense. There's a whole folder of stuff he's got to work with. Shit.

"All right."

Missa doesn't look at me. Her left hand clenches a knife, the blade blurring as she slices, chops, and dices. Salad.

"We need to do a scrub."

This time she glances at me, an unspoken question on her face.

I answer it. "We need to scrub the Manor. Get rid of everything with connections to the business. Make it a showroom in here. The girls can highlight some textbooks, leave laptops out with their online classes pulled up, and do "study groups" out back. We can leave old drafts of the travel guides out. We've already got the ones in the living room, but I'm thinking we can really sell the 'educational writing group' thing."

Missa dumps a cutting board full of fruit and veggies into a massive wooden bowl, rinses her hands, dries them on a kitchen towel, and turns to me. "I should hope so. That's kinda the whole point."

I stick out my tongue.

"Really, though." Her tone turns serious. "Where are we moving everything? There are the false bottoms in the sitting room. The hidden closet in the foyer." She clicks her tongue and glances up. "The attic."

I nod, these all crossed my mind. "We don't have much that needs hiding. Documentation and the guns that aren't registered—actually, maybe all the guns. Everything else pretty much can stay out. We just have to set it up so the Manor looks more like a school than it does now."

"You wanna go all X-Men Academy on their ass."

"I was thinking Hogwarts. But sure, we can go X-Men."

She exhales a chuckle and sits across from me. "We can make that happen. Won't even take much work." She pauses, then asks in a worried tone, "Do you really think McKinley's gonna get into the Manor?"

A shiver goes through me. The idea of a cadre of cops storming through my—our—home, overturning furniture, rifling through drawers, hassling my girls, heats up my temper.

"No," I lie. It's a little lie. The truth is that I don't know. I have no idea and that's what scares me the most. "Better safe than sorry. Plus, I know you'd rather do all this than go talk to—"

"Ugh," she interrupts, putting a hand up and glaring at me. "Don't even start with that. He is a *last* resort. *Last.* I'm not talking to him unless we are absolutely fucked."

My hands go up in a "don't kill me" defensive gesture, but I can't keep the laugh erupting from my throat.

A bright pink head, yet again, pokes around the wall to the living room. "Was he really that bad?"

Missa shoves away from the table as my laughter transforms into a fit of giggles. She points a finger at me.

"Last resort."

Josie looks from Missa, now turning back to her nasty salad, to me, almost falling out of my chair. "That's bad." Her head bobs in a nod. "Okay. What's for lunch?"

She sticks her head around Missa's arm, catches sight of the kale (which is ruining a perfectly delicious collection of chicken, fruit, veggies, and cheese) and backs out of the room with a grin.

"Never mind! I'm not hungry."

"It's healthy for you, dammit," Missa shouts after her. Missa spears a chunk of kale and chicken and plops it into her mouth.

My stomach aches from laughing and each inhale sends a dull—yet strong—burst of pain through my chest. Worth it for the look on Missa's face as she turns to me, pointing the empty fork menacingly at my head and talking with her mouth full.

"You turned them all against me. Kale is good for you."

"Sorry, babe," I say. I back away from the table, side-eyeing my exit. "If it helps, I didn't turn them against *you*, just against the green devil." I flash a grin and slip from the kitchen. Time to shower and then get some work done.

Chapter Six

Damen

Awkward

"**A**re you going to call them, at least?"

I sip from my vanilla latte to avoid answering Gabe's question. It's Tuesday morning. We're at brunch, enjoying the delicious cuisine at Don Mamino in Miraflores. It's a gorgeous little restaurant. The display case tempts me to collect about a dozen sweets for my drive to Arequipa.

If I wanted to, I could gather a bunch of goodies and go visit my family. Take my little sister something with strawberries. They'd still be her favorite, right? And chocolate for Carmen, vanilla for Mama.

Unless everything they like is different after three years.

"Not yet."

Gabe rolls his eyes.

"I have to take care of this," I murmur.

"But you won't tell me what 'this' is?"

I shake my head, and Gabe takes a frustrated bite from his breakfast empanada.

"I don't want to get you involved. I'm taking care of something that should have been dealt with three years ago."

"And when you're done," he mumbles, swallows, and speaks clearly this time, "you'll be able to come and go as you please? Visit more often? Move back to Peru?"

I warm my fingers on my mug. A plate of eggs, bacon, and a biscuit sits before me, but the minute the food came out, my stomach roiled. It happens tomorrow night. Probably.

I spent most of yesterday—once I got back to Lima from Señora Luccela's—prepping. Research, making calls, putting on my best American accent. Buccero has made that office building in San Isidro the headquarters for his company. Five years ago, all he wanted to do was hide behind shell companies. Maintain his influence over the president and keep his business making money without him doing much work.

Things have changed.

There is a new president. Courtesy of Miss Belle and myself three years ago stopping the incumbent from backroom dealing his way into a rigged election. Buccero won't have any luck on the political side of things—especially not fresh out of prison. He's CEO again. A title that didn't leave during his prison sentence, likely because of all the shell companies.

Instead, Buccero's focus is expanding his company. Spreading his influence like a rot. A disease eating away at Peru.

Buccero doesn't like to sleep where he works, this I know from my time as his assistant. Records show a recently purchased villa just outside of Arequipa. A gorgeous estate, set apart from the other wealthy homes in that area. His sprawls just on the other side of a ribbon-like stream, flowing past the edge of the city.

If his assistant's most recent interview is true, Buccero will be there tomorrow night.

Gabe clears his throat.

"Yes." I straighten, my gaze flicking through the restaurant. I focus on my friend. "I won't be moving back, but I'll be able to visit more."

Gabe nods. "And you'll give me a heads-up next time? So, I can take a few days off work, and we can really get into it? I have some clubs to take you to."

I laugh. "Are we dragging my sister along?"

Gabe flushes. "Listen, about that..."

I put up a hand. "If you two are starting things up again, I'm not sure I want to know."

"It's not like that at all." Gabe swirls the dregs of his coffee in his mug. "She reached out a few weeks ago about my major."

My brow furrows. "Photography, right?"

He nods again. "I plan on making a career of it, but not for a while. I love the hostel. The people, the drinks, the hours. Plus, I'm getting plenty of photos there. Lots of practice."

I grin. "You don't have to convince me."

Gabe chuckles. "Sorry, my Ma has been... unhappy about my work choices. Anyway, Carmen called me out of the blue about three weeks ago and asked if I could make it up to Cuzco."

"What?" I frown and lean in.

"Yeah, she's been running protests along the Amazon. There's a company trying to steal the land out from under the Quechua people. They want to burn it all down and turn it into cattle ranching, coffee and cocoa fields, all that shit."

I rub the bridge of my nose. "She wants you to take pictures to get more publicity?"

"Yep. I'm taking four days off starting next Thursday."

My head bobs in a gentle nod. "That's kind of you."

Gabe shrugs. His face grows red again. "I... I feel like I fucked it up between us all when she broke things off. I shouldn't have reacted the way I did."

A half-smile twitches across my lips. We'd been friends for years. Grew up in the same small town outside of Lima, went on church trips together, took classes together... The three of us were near inseparable.

Carmen and Gabe started dating a few months before we all graduated, but it didn't last long. He fell hard and fast, and my sister, not so much. He didn't come around after she ended things. Then I got the job in the city and...

"It's not entirely your fault," I say. "I started working a few weeks after the break-up and I was barely around at that point. We just..."

"Fell apart?"

I nod.

Gabe picks a slice of bacon off my untouched plate. "I'm glad you're back. When you get done with your secret mission," he wiggles his eyebrows and I glare, "the three of us should go for coffee."

"That sounds great."

The drive from Lima to Arequipa is sixteen hours in the right traffic. I'd fly if it weren't for the duffle of highly illegal firearms on the floor of the backseat. It's buried under a few beach blankets and my normal go-bag.

Instead of flying, I pray for light traffic and limited tourists. I'll have to stop on the way; I don't need to be there until Wednesday night. Fortunately, the 1S follows the coast most of the way and, between the sprawling homes surrounding Lima, I have a gorgeous view of the ocean.

It takes an hour to get through the constantly expanding outskirts of Lima. The city just keeps growing.

My mind slips. Glides away from the scenery before me and shifts to the reason I had to leave.

The money was so good. Enough to guarantee my college tuition after just a year. I took bundles of cash back to Mama when I went home for Sunday morning mass. I was learning a lot about the inner workings of Peru's politics. It felt like opportunities were opening before me.

I ignored the rumors. Buccero had gone through six executive assistants in two years. But those boys were younger than me. From small villages in central Peru. Not used to the big city. The pressure.

I thought I was different.

Along with those rumors came better ones. Buccero was known for helping people up the ladder. Those assistants, receptionists, maids—everyone who worked for him found better things waiting for them when the time came to move on.

I'd talked Carmen into applying for a summer internship just before it happened the first time. When I went home that weekend, she didn't understand why I ripped the paper up. Why I shouted at her. Told her she wouldn't get in anyway and brought her nearly to tears before I stormed out of the house.

We got over it. My twin and I got through that fight and a handful of others that popped up over those two years.

After Miss Belle approached me, after it all came to a head and I'd had enough and would do almost anything to get away... after I confessed it all to Carmen, in the middle of the night on the floor of Mama's kitchen, hushed tones and muffled sobs, I watched realization click into place in her eyes.

When I murmured how sorry I was, she hugged me. We held each other. Like we had after Papa died.

Then she brushed away my tears and told me to accept Miss Belle's offer. I don't think either of us realized what that would mean.

I jerk the steering wheel to avoid a hole in the road and focus my mind. There is work to be done.

I spend a few hours planning it out in my head, then I distract myself with music. An hour after sunset I take a right and zip back toward the coast to Puerto De Lomas. The little fishing beach village reminds me of home.

Tourists chatter in the street as I scoot my car to Hotel Lomas Beach. Clean, bright, with fresh smelling sheets and a stunning view of the ocean. I pay for the night, dump all my bags in the room, and order some food.

My muscles are tight and sore from the drive, and I have another eight hours to go tomorrow. A bit less since Buccero's compound is on the northern side of Arequipa, cutting down the drive because I don't have to go through the vast city to reach him.

My lips curl around the beer I'm sipping. The anger, the hatred in my heart, doesn't feel like it belongs. I set the bottle down with a clunk and close my eyes. The sound of the ocean crashes to my left.

I unclench my hand, fingers stiff, and run my thumb along my cross. I need strength tonight, the strength to sleep without nightmares, to wake with no falter in my resolution.

I murmur under my breath, lips shaping a prayer from memory, "*You will call on me and come and pray to me, and I will listen to you.*"

I go to bed early, and when I wake in the morning, it seems God heard me. My rest was deep and dark, no dreams of any kind that I remember.

The girl at the front counter takes my key with a smile and offers an umbrella for the beach. I turn her down kindly, glancing out at the sand, already spotted with rainbow umbrellas. The sun has barely come up, but tourists are crowding the shore. It's not water weather in the Southern Hemisphere, but the sand will warm up soon enough.

I wish I could stay. Get Em down here and do nothing but swing in a hammock with her for a few days. She deserves a vacation.

I fill my gas tank on the way out of town, grab a handful of snacks, and try to mentally prepare myself for the next eight hours and what will come after.

If you have the opportunity, and confidence, to rent a car and drive, do it. There are so many places tourists miss out on because they only fly and take cabs. Take San Fernando National Reserve for example. This sprawling reserve along the coast of Peru has stunning views of the ocean. Photographers spend hours nailing the perfect shot of ocean spray. The coastline of Peru is littered with adorable villages and towns, beaches ready for sand-castle-making, and restaurants with some of the best seafood you'll ever eat.

Driving in a foreign country is nerve-wracking. It's important to do some research. Figure out which side of the road people drive on, double-check that your license works in said country, and make sure you get a reliable car rental. Once you've dotted your Ps and Qs, have fun, be safe, and enjoy your adventure.

Also make sure to take all of your belongings out of the car when you stop for the night. Especially if you have anything questionable in the back.

Chapter Seven

Damen

The Words Between Us

I park on a shadowed side-street. Close to the river, near a park still echoing with laughter of children playing. The sun falls to the horizon quickly, casting everything in red and orange light. I turn off the car, lean my head against the seat, and breathe for a few minutes.

When I open my eyes, the families have left. Returned to their homes. Settled in for a night of dinner, television, games, sleep...

I step out of the car and stretch.

I arrived on the outskirts of Arequipa a little while ago. The evening darkness is what I've been waiting for. The stillness of a wealthy area after nightfall.

I pop the trunk, pull out my medium-sized bag, and get ready. A vest under my black sweater. Gun at my ankle, my hip. A silencer in one of my deeper pants pockets. I lace the boots up tight, the handle of a blade barely poking out the top of the right one. Another blade goes on my left inner arm, strapped in place under my sleeve. I pull down the ski-cap. Not a full-face version like a clichéd bank thief, a regular hat that keeps my head warm and covers the tips of my ears.

A few more supplies adorn my belt. When I'm finally ready, I stretch and lock up the car.

My heartbeat thunders in my ears as the adrenaline kicks up. I haven't even done anything yet.

I can't get Em's voice out of my head. *I don't want it to be like this.*

I don't either.

With a sigh, I yank open the passenger door and pull my cell from the glove box. Regular mission or not, it feels odd and dangerous to have my civilian phone on me. Still, I told her I'd call.

Now may be the only time.

The phone rings three times before she picks up. "Damen?"

"Hey, *bonita.*"

A light chuckle. "I'm glad you called. How are things going?"

My chest contracts. This was a bad idea. I can't tell her *anything.* "It's..." My mind whirls. "It's going all right. Turns out there is a chance to collect some art while I handle the family stuff."

"That's amazing." The genuine excitement in her voice cracks my heart. "I expect some pictures when you get back," she says with a laugh.

"Absolutely. How are you?" My gaze moves from the scratch on the car I've been staring at. I look out across the river choked with vegetation.

"Good. I started sketching a new design last night. Made some real progress before class started this morning."

"That's great." I'm distracted. I hear it in my own voice as my thoughts take a darker turn. She hears it too.

"Are you sure you're okay?"

"Yeah, just... I just called to hear your voice, check in. I have to go."

There is just enough sadness in her tone that I know I've disappointed her. "Right. I appreciate it. I miss you."

"I miss you too."

There is a pause. Unspoken words thrown into the night sky between Peru and New York.

"Night," I choke out.

She says it back just as I hang up.

I curse under my breath, chuck the phone back into the glove compartment, and re-lock the car.

"That wasn't smart," I mutter to myself as I start my trek.

I walk up the road, following the river upstream until I reach a stone and brick carved bridge. On my side, mansion homes sit on half-acre lots. Wrought-iron fences, glistening white-pickets, pillars of marble, glass-stained windows, and cascading immaculate lawns as far as the eye can see. Beyond them, on the edge of the horizon, light from Arequipa glows against the black sky.

On the far side of the bridge sit the villas. The homes of ridiculous wealth. High stone walls. Courtyards filled with fountains and trees. Guards. Guns. Protection.

There's a camera on the bridge. It faces the road, watching for suspicious individuals driving across.

Someone stupid put up a few pictures online: images to sell rich tourists on visiting Arequipa. I know the angle of the camera.

I stride into the vegetation along the side of the bridge. Crossing through the water is a possibility but feels foolish. The river is deep. Fast flowing. And I'd be all wet.

Instead, I get a few yards past the beginning of the bridge, just before the arc of stone lifts over the water. I back up, take a running start, and leap. My fingers grasp the edges of stone.

I heave. Pull myself up the side and, with a silent grunt, scoot my body onto the ornate raised edge of the bridge.

I lay on the stone, panting for a brief second. Then I scurry to my feet and, balancing along the edge, walk across the bridge.

I drop down on the other side with a map in my mind, anxiety in my stomach, and pounding in my heart.

It's still early. The sun has set, but plenty of lights are on, both in the villas before me and in the homes across the river.

Buccero's villa is one of the newest. Close to the bridge.

A paved road follows the river along the outside edge of the villas, darting inward every now and then to take someone to a gated driveway. I stick to the far side. Vegetation hides me from any eyes peeping out of windows.

Buccero's front gate comes into view after a minute of walking. The curved iron is open, the gates themselves propped against towering brick walls. Inside, flickers of light come from massive windows, maybe thirty yards from the entrance. Two guards patrol the wall. One rounds a corner and strides toward the gate.

I duck into the bushes, taking a slow and careful step back. The guard stops for a moment, takes a puff from a cigarette, and then continues on his way.

A third man sits on a tall stool just inside the gate. He checks his watch, heaves a sigh, and stands. With lumbering movements, he paces out to the gate and closes one side, then the other.

I inhale, flexing my hands—careful not to crack my knuckles—and mouthing a prayer. Then I settle in for a long wait.

Tonight, Buccero dies. I won't risk that promise by rushing things.

Chapter Eight

Miss Belle

Early Morning Electricians

Shapes move toward me. Faces in the dark. Faces familiar to me... but why?

I take a step back as realization hits me, but my foot touches nothing. I fall, arms whirling, a scream wrenching through my throat. I hit something like water. But water isn't this heavy.

I splutter and cough, trying to swim to shore. There is no shore. I paddle desperately against the current. Something grabs at my legs. Something pulls me down. Again and again and again. I stare through dark red liquid. What has me?

Through the haze, I see them again. The faces. They swim toward me. First the ones I killed directly. The men from Thailand, the Russian, the warlord near Zambia, the cartel soldiers... then come the ones I was responsible for. The ones I couldn't save.

My muscles ache from the effort of escaping them. Fear clogs my veins, my blood doesn't pump right. Pressure builds in my chest, higher and higher, until I snap and inhale, blood rushing into my lungs.

Blistering pain wakes me. I would normally jump out of bed, but my limbs seem frozen in place. The pressure is still there, in my chest, drowning me.

No.

I blink, wincing.

It's not pressure, it's just bruised ribs. I must have slept at a weird angle.

I'm not drowning.

I press my palms against my closed eyes until red blotches cover my vision. A sharp pain throbs behind my right eye. My neck aches.

With a groan, I pull the pale blue sheet off my body, roll to the side, and push myself up. My bedside table, a little wooden thing with a single drawer and a stack of books on the bottom shelf, isn't quite where it goes. I must have been thrashing.

A glance at the pillows on the floor confirms this. I move the table back where it goes, and squint at the sky-blue hand-clock on its surface.

7:00a.m. I rub my face again, not as hard this time, and stand up.

The slice in my back itches. I make a mental note to have Missa double check and make sure it's still healing properly. Then, hand pressed to my ribs in a futile effort to stem the steady pain that comes from too much physical activity—or breathing—I make my way to the closet and get dressed.

Half an hour later, I'm clambering down the stairs, into the foyer, and on to the kitchen. In my sleepy-but-can't-sleep-cuz-dreams-suck state of mind, I almost don't notice the first knock at the door. It's only after I've started tapping the counter that I realize I'm tapping after each knock. Like a crazy person.

I shuffle from the kitchen, glad I put on clothes rather than just a robe, and back to the foyer.

A figure stands on the other side of the ornate wooden front door. His outline is visible through the stained glass. Tall, well built—or maybe husky—hard to tell from the outline. Either way, I glance around before opening the door.

On the long table we use for keys, mail, and a very cute vase Jeanette brought back from Poland one time, sits our letter-opener.

I snatch it up and slip it into my back pocket, handle easily accessible. Then, one hand tucked into that same pocket in a super casual stance, I unlock the door and open it a crack.

"Good morning, ma'am."

I wince. He probably doesn't mean to be so loud, but it's the morning, goddamn it. This is the time for the sounds of birds chirping, coffee-makers dripping, and perhaps the sizzle of bacon on a pan.

It's not the time for a half-giant to be barking down at me from my threshold.

"Good morning," I manage to get out in a less gravely tone than I feared. "What can I do for you at this... early hour?" I cock my head with that half-smile that says something a little less polite than my actual words.

"Yeah, sorry about that." The giant shuffles his feet and gives an apologetic grin.

He is quite tall, must be at least 6 '2". With a scruffy red beard and mustache, hair to match, and vibrant blue eyes, he looks like an Irishman far from home. Born in the States though, based on the light Midwestern lilt.

I give him a once-over, taking in a black baseball cap, thick denim jeans—the kind laborers wear—a toolkit in his left hand, a utility belt hanging loosely from his waist, and the unnecessarily tight shirt which shows more of his muscular definition than I need to be seeing before I've had my coffee.

He's talking. Shit. Pay attention.

"—definitely not my idea to be up here so early in the morning. They've had me knocking on doors since 6:30, and let me tell you, people are not happy. The main office'll be getting calls all day. I'm sure of it. But, not my problem at this point. I just do what I'm told and poor Jenny down at corporate will have to deal with the fallout." He gives me another grin and shakes his head, like I should understand about Jenny and the phone calls and whatnot.

"Right..." I blink hard and try to focus. My back itches. "So, what are you here for?"

The words come out before I realize how rude they are, but the man doesn't seem to notice.

"I've got to get a look at your electric."

"My electric what?"

He pauses, then slowly holds up the toolkit. "Your electric box, ma'am. Out back? We've had some funny readings in the neighborhood, and I'm supposed to do a reset of every box on the block by 9am."

I squint at him, my mouth hanging a little open, a strong desire to shut the door quickly overwhelming me.

"Paperwork?"

"What?" He leans forward and raises an eyebrow.

I say it again, louder.

"Ope, of course!" There's that grin again. He plunks the toolbox on the ground, pops it open, and pulls out a set of documents folded into thirds. "Let's see... number... there we are."

He hands me a sheet of paper with an official looking electric company seal at the top. It's a short paragraph apologizing for the interruption and requesting permission for a serviceman to take a look at the box. There is a number at the bottom for questions. And it's signed by Jenny.

"Uh... okay. So, you need, what? Access to the backyard?"

He nods and heaves a relieved sigh. "Thanks for being so understanding. I don't get why they have me out here so early. Must be to try and catch folks before they go to work."

I nod mutely and open the door further. As he steps onto the plush green carpet that stretches across the hardwood from the front door to the end of the foyer, I poke my head outside and give the street a quick scan. Apart from the old blue pick-up, there are no odd-looking vehicles. Looks like McKinnley is still missing. Good.

I shut the door, my hand still in the back pocket next to the letter opener. I toss the paper onto the table and gesture for the man to continue forward.

"Back door is through here."

"Thanks again," he says as he takes hesitant steps through the house. "You can call me Jake, by the way. Sorry for not introducing myself earlier. I've had a lot of doors shut in my face this morning. Guess I was surprised by your helpfulness."

"Yeah, well, you're just doing your job, right?" I mumble. My body is ready for caffeine. My mind is ready to get this guy into the backyard and out of my house. And the part of me that isn't dying of hunger, sleep deprivation, and physical pain, thinks I should take him upstairs and find out whether or not he skips leg day.

"Yep. I'll try to be done before you have to get the kids to school."

That completely throws me.

"What?"

Jake gestures to the piles of textbooks, notebooks, and highlighters scattered throughout the living room.

"Oh." I shake my head. "No, I don't have any kids. I run a college program for people interested in travel, journalism, and writing. The classes are all online, but a lot of the students live here. Makes it easier to collaborate."

He nods, taking a closer look at the textbooks. "Ahh, that makes sense. Very neat. Also explains the advanced language classes and..."

I follow his gaze and clamp my teeth down on my tongue. Sarah left out her stack of dominatrix guides. The top book has a cover photo demonstrating what I can only imagine is a purposefully painful time for everyone involved.

"Ha-ha." My forced chuckle squeaks from my lips, and I awkwardly step between the books and his line of sight. "People sure do have some weird interests. But everyone is allowed to follow their own hobbies outside of classes."

I laugh again, and Jake gives me a weak smile.

"Backyard is right through here." I gesture and nod.

He turns away from the living room—thank God—and I try to remember if there is anything suspicious laying around in the kitchen as well. Fortunately, there is not. The only dastardly things are a massive Ninja blender on the counter and the row of brand-new skillets I bought Sarah for her birthday last week hanging along the wall.

I push open the backdoor, walk him down the little stone path that leads to the garage, veer down a second path that takes us around the edge of the house, and present him with the back yard.

I wouldn't say I'm heavily into gardening. I enjoy the outdoors as much as any other California girl, but New York gets cold in the winter and humid in the summer, and I just don't have the patience necessary to wait for seeds to germinate, for plants to grow, for fruit to ripen.

It's possible I got in trouble a few times last fall for picking the apples too early and ruining Sarah's plans for apple tarts. Though I'm pretty sure I was the one most upset by the loss of the tarts.

The back yard isn't as much my space as some of the other girls. But damn if it isn't beautiful.

A wooden fence, dark brown and eight feet tall, lines the back portion of the Manor property. The backyard extends from behind the main house, across the little stretch of open land, and on behind the garage. Winding stone-step pathways lead from the kitchen door to the garage door and to the massive oak in the far corner with a swinging bench underneath it. The steps trail through the middle of the yard, taking one along the edge of the massive, raised beds, beautiful set of fountains, and to the two-person hammock which dangles between two trees on the opposite side of the oak. A small gazebo, dark wood matching the fence, is nestled in the space behind the garage and has seating for another few people.

Jake's breath whooshes out, and a rush of pride goes through my chest.

"Wow."

I glance at him. He gazes around the yard, eyes trying to take in every little detail. He grins at the fairy lights dangling from the house to the trees. A deep chuckle tickles out when he catches sight of the miniature fairy doors, bridges, and furniture Josie and Alex have tucked into almost every corner.

He slaps a hand on the wooden picnic table and turns to me, eyes wide.

"This is amazing."

I give a nod of thanks. "It really is. I can't take credit for it though. The gir—the students, spend a lot of time and energy making this place awesome."

"I always wanted a yard like this. My Grandma had a big ol' yard. We spent almost all our summers at her farm in Kansas."

Midwest. I was right.

"Yeah, well, anyway." I stifle a yawn and point at a spot just next to the kitchen window. "There's the reader and the box. I'm going back in for some coffee."

He nods and gives me a "thank you." I've opened the door and stepped inside when a flash of my father's voice blares through my head, admonishing me for having horrid manners.

I stick my head back outside.

"Can I get you anything to drink?"

"Oh, um... Yeah, a coffee would be great."

"Cream or sugar?" I grumble.

"Both. A lot of both. Thanks."

I roll my eyes as the door closes behind me. Honestly. Why even get a coffee if you're going to drown it with cream and sugar?

"GAHH!"

My heart leaps from my chest, lodges in my throat, and proceeds to beat insanely loudly in my ears.

Missa gives me a mild stare from her perch leaned against the kitchen counter. "Oh, sorry. Did I scare you?"

I glare at her, still breathing fast.

"No, I was just getting in my morning scream. You ass."

The kitchen door opens once again, and Jake's concerned face pokes in.

"Everything okay?"

"Yep. I'll bring out your coffee in a minute." I give a tight smile as Jake's gaze moves to Missa.

"Morning, ma'am."

My jaw doesn't exactly drop, but Jake's lack of drooling over Missa in her pajamas is a bit of a shock. Maybe he's waiting to fall into a coma until he's out of sight.

He gives a curt nod, shuts the door, and we soon hear the tell-tale sounds of metal tools clanging together and someone messing with the side of the house.

Missa watches me, one immaculate eyebrow raised.

I ignore her and make my way to the coffee pot. After hitting some buttons—admittedly a little harder than they needed hitting—I grab mugs from the cupboard, sugar from the little jar on the counter, cream from the fridge, and stand, staring at the coffee machine.

"Ahem," Missa clears her throat.

I give her a glance.

"Who the fuck is that?" she asks.

"Some guy with the electric company. He's doing... something about checking a box..." I wave my hand through the air. "Stuff. I don't know. He had paperwork."

She gives me a deadpan stare.

"What?"

"You don't think that's a little odd?"

"What's a little odd?"

"Oh, I don't know..." Missa goes to the freezer and pulls out a bowl of pre-chopped fruits. "It's a little odd that..." With a grunt, she plops the bowl on the counter. She opens the fridge without looking and—while staring at me—grabs out the orange juice and plain yogurt. "Someone shows up the day after McKinnley halts surveillance and claims to need access to the back of the house."

I cross my arms, irritated and embarrassed that I hadn't thought of that.

"He had paperwork confirming that he's supposed to be here. From the electric company."

She plugs in the beast that is the blender and begins to assemble her smoothie.

"Right." A plop and a splash as two whole bananas and a bit of orange juice settle between the blades. "Because it's entirely impossible for the cops to fake something like that to gain access to our home." Several handfuls of spinach, cubes of frozen peaches, strawberries, blueberries, and other things I'm too distracted to identify.

"So, you think..."

"Yes. I think that man is a cop. And," she shakes her head at me, "I think you're totally useless in the morning."

She starts the blender before I can respond. I focus on the coffee maker which has just started its shrill beeping. I pour "Jake," if that is his real name, half a mug-full of the nearly black, insanely rich coffee. Several spoonfuls of sugar and nearly half a cup of cream turn the color a swirling milky beige.

Gross.

I clench the mug in shaking hands. I shouldn't be so angry. If he's a cop, he's just doing his job. If he's not a cop, well then, he's really just doing his job. Either way, it's my fault for letting him into the house.

Missa is right. I'm useless in the morning.

I shove open the kitchen door and stalk outside. Before rounding the corner of the house, I force my lips into a calm, serene smile. Basically what I picture my face to look like after I've had eight hours of sleep, a long shower, coffee, and eggs, and plenty of time in the morning to read the paper.

None of those things have happened this morning, so I'm doubtful that my face looks the way I want. Still, it's better than glowering at him. Especially if he's a cop.

"Here you go!" I smile wider, my teeth clenching hard.

"Ahh, excellent." Jake turns from the open metal box and sets his screwdriver on the table.

I hand him the mug. He sips. I get no joy from his facial expression. I was hoping he'd wince at the stupidly sweet flavor from the ridiculous amount of cream and sugar I put in.

"Perfect," he murmurs, mug still at his lips. "Thank you."

"Of course. Happy to do it."

We stand in silence for a moment. I glance into the kitchen window. Missa is rinsing out the blender, watching us closely.

"How does my box look?"

Jake splutters, coffee dribbling down his scruffy chin. "Uh..." he stutters. His gaze moves from me to the electric box, and he nods quickly.

I'd feel embarrassment, but I'm fresh outta fucks.

"It's great, um, looking good. Doesn't seem to be a problem with the output or the numbers."

He keeps talking, says some technical stuff, and I keep my gaze locked on his face, searching for the lie.

"How much longer do you have out here?"

"Oh, just a few more minutes. I've got to check one more thing then I'll close her up and be on my way."

I nod. "Just knock on that kitchen door when you're done, and I'll walk you back out."

He grins and raises the coffee in a salute.

I go back into the kitchen.

"Well?" Missa hands me a mug of coffee—black, the way it should be drunk.

"I don't know. He didn't look like he was lying. When he leaves, we should have Anita see if there's anything funky with the wires."

Anita, currently twisting her black wavy hair into neat braids at the end of the kitchen table, nods. "Morning, Miss Belle."

"Hey, babe. You get any coffee yet?"

She wrinkles her slender nose, full lips curling up to show her dazzlingly straight teeth. "Never."

I roll my eyes as Missa laughs and sets a wine glass full of smoothie on the table next to our little Latina.

"I can't believe you let some random guy walk through the house," Anita says. She takes a sip of the smoothie, leaving a pink trail across her upper lip, and gives Missa a thank you nod and smile.

Josie saunters around the corner and plops down next to Anita. "She did what?"

I sigh and sit in my usual chair at the head of the table.

"Come look," Missa whispers loudly. She waves an impatient hand at Josie, and the pixie-looking girl leaves her chair to join Missa at the window.

"Ohh, I kinda get why you let him in."

Anita snorts and Missa's shoulders shake with laughter.

I glower at them and take a loud slurping sip of my coffee. "It's early, I didn't sleep well, and he had the proper paperwork!"

There's a knock at the kitchen door, and we all freeze, staring at the silhouette behind the panes.

"Oh, for fuck's sake." I stand, open the kitchen door, and gesture for Jake to come on in.

His eyes widen at the sight of three beautiful women staring at him. I am not staring at him. I'm glaring at my girls.

"Good morning. Thanks for letting me get this all taken care of. Y'all have been the nicest house so far by a long shot."

Missa nods warmly and thanks him for making sure everything looks right with our electricity. Anita watches him passively, and Josie bounces a bit on the balls of her feet.

"Right, well, we should get you on your way," I say in a sing-song voice.

Missa hides her smile with her own glass of smoothie, and I gesture for Jake to move through the kitchen.

I glance back as we turn the corner into the living room and catch all three women staring after me with annoying smirks on their smug faces.

I shake my head, bite my lip, and follow Jake through the house to the front door.

"So, everything is done? You won't need to come back to check anything?"

"Uh." His gaze darts to the left.

I frown.

"No, no, probably not. I can't see any reason for me to need to come back."

"All right then, goodbye!"

I shut the door, leaving him standing on the front porch with a slightly put-out facial expression.

A deep pull of oxygen fills my lungs. I lock the door and turn from Jake's silhouette.

"Anita!" I shout; a pang goes through my chest, and I wince.

"On it." Comes the reply.

I trudge back to the kitchen, running a hand through my loose hair and heaving several sighs.

Josie sits in her chair at the table, sipping her weirdly fancy glass of smoothie. Anita's dark hair can be spotted through the window as she examines whatever Jake did. Missa stands at the stove, three frying pans in front of her, simultaneously cooking strips of turkey bacon, eggs, and blueberry pancakes.

My stomach churns at the sight. I should be hungry, but all I feel at the moment is nausea and anxiety. My fingers press against my eyes. It's too much.

Something slams with a bang and I jerk up, fear lacing my veins, heart pounding, chest heaving.

My right hand clenches and unclenches.

Where is it?

It was right here. My gun.

No.

No, that's not right. I don't have my gun. I don't need my gun. I flatten my hand on the surface of the table and press down. My right hand is secure against the wood; my left shakes like a leaf.

Josie hasn't noticed. Dimly, I am aware of her chattering away about some fluff piece she read on a news site.

Missa though...

My oldest friend stares at me from her station next to the stove. She holds a spatula in one hand, grease dripping from the edge and plunking onto the counter.

She catches my gaze and doesn't look away. Her pale blue eyes bore into me, reading far more than I want to share.

I swallow. I pry up my right hand and clench both around my coffee mug. Without being able to properly say why, I look away, shame filling me. After another moment, and a faint smell of burning becomes apparent, Missa turns back to her breakfast foods and flips a pancake.

Anita returns a few minutes later, her usually jovial face creased in a serious and telling frown.

"What is it?"

"Nothing good." Her mix of Mexican and Cuban accents dances through the words, becoming clearer when she is agitated (like now, for instance). "Missa was right. No way that guy was an electrician."

I exhale and rub my temple. "What makes you say that?"

"The listening device for starters."

Missa drops her spatula, Josie chokes on her smoothie, and I stare at Anita.

She nods. "He connected it to the house, so it doesn't have to run on a battery. It's a long-term device. They don't have to recharge it or bring a new one. It's designed specifically for extended recon missions."

I grind my teeth. "What's the range? Can he hear us now?" My brow furrows, matching my frown.

"No." She gives me a wry look. "I'm not dumb enough to talk about it if they can hear us. It's an outdoor mic. It will pick up pretty much every sound in the backyard, but it can't go through walls." She shakes her head. "We probably shouldn't leave the kitchen window or door open though."

She snags a plate, stacks a few pancakes, strips of bacon, and spoonfuls of eggs, and plunks herself back into her seat at the table.

"That explains the van being gone." Missa looks at me. "McKinnley got a new warrant."

I nod. "And Captain Wallace owes me a fruit basket."

"With muffins!" Josie chimes in.

Chapter Nine

Damen

A Murder

Night closes in around me. Light from the city is far enough that the stars are visible, twinkling above me.

According to that last interview, Buccero is going to arrive in Lima in two days. He's here. In his villa, surrounded by walls and guards. Comfortable. Safe.

I bring my delicate golden cross to my lips before tucking it into my shirt.

I stride through the vegetation, moving past Buccero's villa and circling the estate next to his. It's owned by a movie star off on a film set in Miami. The place is deserted, leaving me a nice buffer of darkness between my trek and Buccero's place.

Before too long, I've reached the back wall. Another few seconds and the guards will turn that corner, circle around, and disappear again. I wait, crouched at his neighbor's wall. The gap between the brick barriers is about fifteen feet wide.

The second the guards are out of sight, I spring to my feet and rush to the wall. I unfurl the rope at my side, attach a cloth covered grapple to the end, and fling it up.

The cloth muffles a thud as the metal tongs hit the far side of the twelve-foot-tall brick wall. I jerk the rope. It doesn't budge.

I pull, hefting my weight and plant my feet on the bricks ahead of me.

This took some getting used to. During my year of training, the obstacles involving height, especially having to go nearly horizontal while climbing a wall, gave me the most trouble.

I prefer staying inside and looking at art.

With a grunt, I reach the top of the wall and crawl myself onto the foot-wide ledge. Lying on my back, I detach the grapple, reattach it to the outside edge, and use the rope to lower myself down the other side. Going down is much faster than going up.

Once I hit the bottom, I give the rope a few flicks. Without much effort the grapple releases. I catch it as it falls.

My escape plan is the same as my entrance. With any luck, I'll be in and out of the massive stucco building where Buccero lives without anyone noticing. A bullet in the heart. One in the head for good measure.

Then I will scurry back here, go over the wall, and begin the work of dumping weapons and getting back to Lima to establish an alibi with Gabe.

I suck in a cool breath of air. Above me, clouds form, blocking the stars.

The villa garden is pristine. A winding path of gravel is lined with evenly trimmed grass. Trees decorate the lawn, none tall enough or close enough to the wall to help with getting in or out. Young saplings, recently planted.

The back of the house is about sixty yards from where I climbed over. A marble lined pool, water shimmering with light from the occasional break in the clouds, sits against the back patio. Everything here is expensive. The best materials and contractors money can buy.

Hanging orbs of light decorate the dark wooden pergola that stretches out from the house, stopping just before the edge of the water.

My time spent researching public blueprints yesterday wasn't a waste. Beyond the pool is a back door made of glass with light wood trim; it matches all the windows along the back wall of the house. I'm in the shadows, ducking around trees and bushes, and still I feel exposed.

That door is a dangerous option. Too much light.

Instead, I skirt around the edge of the house to find a side door, one that leads directly to the kitchen. Essentially a servant's entrance. There so Buccero doesn't have to witness his guards coming and going, his cooks and maids arriving for their shifts. So he can pretend he's the self-made man he claims to be.

After rounding the corner, I come to a sudden halt. I slink up against the side of the house, pressing into shadows.

The gray gravel path leading around both sides of the house in a U-shape is full of cars.

My breath catches, tongue dry as I attempt to swallow down crushing disappointment and fear. These aren't the vehicles of servants. These are wealthy town cars—Lamborghinis and Maseratis.

The side door, over halfway down the house from me, pops open. Light flows onto the ground and sounds greet me from within. Chatter, laughter, music... a man dressed in a crisp white suit with a red and white striped tie and matching vest—looking vaguely similar to the Peruvian flag—steps out. He lights up a cigarette and paces down the row of cars.

The door slams shut behind him.

Taking my time not to make any noise, I step back around the corner of the house and lean my head against the wall. A party. I close my eyes as a rush of frustration and panic heats my chest.

None of the interviews, articles, or company schedules said anything about a party. I imagine Buccero is celebrating his new freedom. He's only been out of prison for a month. Something I found odd, especially since this villa is brand new. Construction finished about six months ago.

The pool is still empty, the patio deserted, likely because of the clouds—now thick and roiling overhead—and the temperature. I don't like the lights.

I slip on a pair of black gloves, thin but with good grips. Keeping myself to the shadows, I hurry along the side of the house. In the dark I want to move slow, keep myself still and hidden. Here, I want to get out of the light as quickly as possible.

I reach for the handle, grasp it, and attempt to turn. I expected it to be unlocked with so many people inside. But the back of the house appears largely deserted. The party must be confined to the massive open foyer, dining, and communal areas I spotted on the blueprints.

Slipping a hand into my back pocket and pulling out a lock-picking kit, I kneel and get to work. It takes almost thirty seconds. My neck itches the whole time. Hairs stand on end as light pours down on me.

My fingers twitch and tremble. I grind my teeth.

A click, and I'm in. I tuck the kit away and silently close the door. Infuriating as it is for Buccero to be living it up in a brand-new villa made just for him, it is nice to not have to worry about old wooden floors creaking under my feet.

If I'd known about the party, I'd have brought a suit. Snuck in, dressed in a closet, hidden my gear, and blended. Well, that's what I've done in the past anyway. I heave a quiet sigh. That wouldn't work here though. Buccero knows my face. If any of his old guards, cronies from his business, or servants from before he went to prison are here, they'd know me too.

I swallow as I reach the end of the darkness. Down the hall ahead of me is an ornately carved staircase, and the foyer of the home. A grand chandelier hangs from the ceiling, glistening with warm yellow light.

The space appears empty. Massive front doors, stained glass window panes consuming the top half of each, rest closed. A function like this, with the caterers and what sounds like live music, would have those doors open until the last guest arrived.

I slink along the edge of the wall, the stair railing above my head. My fingers itch toward the gun at my side. I rest my palm against the grip. I breathe.

Then I clench my jaw, dart around the side of the stairs, and move up as quickly as I can. I have to step over a velvet rope at the bottom, a small sign requesting guests remain on the first floor.

A breath of relief empties my lungs. The second-floor landing is dark. Shadows caused by the delicate chandelier crisscross against a wooden railing that matches the stairs. To the right, a deeper darkness. A black hallway that leads to a collection of bedrooms, bathrooms, and offices.

Given the size of the blueprints, these are for guests and employees Buccero values. None are large enough to be his bedroom.

I veer left and come to a rapid halt, my lungs constricting.

The floor here is carpet, dark and silent, ornate designs of gold woven through. The walls are smooth, cream colored and neutral. Art hangs upon them. Art I recognize, like meeting an old friend after years apart.

I bought these pieces. A Morillo, two by Huanay, and a handful of European artists as well.

Buccero took me to galleries, to museums, to the homes of wealthy collectors. We studied brush strokes, color, and pigments. I learned so much.

My stomach clenches as I reach up a gloved hand and brush the frame I picked out during my first month working in Lima. The painting within is not the high-class, expensive art found on either side. It's a simple piece. Waves crashing against a cliffside. White foam spitting into the sky as the teal water churns. A pale blue sky visible behind thick gray clouds.

Buccero had laughed when I picked it out. It was on the ground in the gallery, pushed against the side of a desk, out of the way. The owner's cousin had painted it.

Buccero bought it anyway. He'd seen it in my eyes, the longing, the craving to see this beautiful display of God's creation as often as possible. He even let me pick out a frame.

My hands shake. I clench them into fists. I close my eyes and picture Arturo's face—the new executive assistant working for Buccero. I picture the way he shifted, a fraction of an inch, when Buccero put a hand on his shoulder.

I remember my flesh crawling each time Buccero touched me. I pull forth the fear, the anger, the hate.

I turn from the paintings and continue down the hallway.

The wall to my right keeps up the expensive art. Occasional long tables carry vases, candles, assortments of fine statues and busts. To my left, the wooden railing continues, lining the hall with pillars set from floor to ceiling every dozen feet.

Below, the foyer has opened into a grand meeting area. I press back, returning to the shadows away from the railing.

Cocktail tables sit in little clusters in the corners and middle of the room. Cushy armchairs take up space next to heavy, dark wood bookshelves full of untouched classics.

People move below me like a dance. Figures in pressed suits, glittering decorations on their ties and cuffs, flowers, feathers, and flared cloth taking the space of pocket squares. Dresses, slick and tight against bodies, or flaring at the breast, waist, and hips, decorate the room in an array of color.

Between them all, white-dressed people move around with golden trays of food, wine, and champagne. One gloved hand holds the bottom of the tray, the other pressed neatly against their lower back. The picture of proper servants.

My gut rumbles as I spot a tray of bacon-wrapped mango. I realize now I didn't eat before I left the car. My last meal was a protein bar on the drive here.

Miss Belle would smack me upside the head if she knew. At least I brought water.

Thoughts of food are driven from my mind as the music—a string quartet in the corner—stops and the man from my nightmares steps to the front of the room. I move behind a nearby pillar and glance around the side, keeping my body in darkness.

"Greetings, friends," Buccero's warm voice, full and deep, caresses the crowd in our native Spanish. "Some of you I've seen recently. But, for most of us, it has been far too long."

A light chuckle goes up through the room. Buccero puts on a good-natured smile.

"Yes, an unfortunate circumstance. Life throws us many challenges, and those of us with the will to do so, rise above."

A smattering of applause.

I swallow the taste of bile on my tongue.

"I want to first offer my congratulations to the members of the city council for our beautiful Arequipa. You've done such lovely things for our city. Expanding territory available for businessmen like myself will bring wonderful new opportunities to Arequipa."

There's louder applause this time. Buccero gestures with his glass, taking a sip of champagne after nodding to a collection of not-quite-as-well-dressed individuals. Still in their finest, but obviously on a city employee's salary—even if it is the highest paying in the city.

Buccero continues. He offers a salute to fellow businessmen, high ranking members of Lima's government—in the opposing party of the sitting president—and representatives of wealthy companies from the United States.

The longer he talks, the more I listen. His assistant refills the champagne as Buccero goes on about zoning regulations near Cuzco. As he thanks a cattle rancher from the States for their input on land management, and for their investment.

My heart thunders against my chest. I came here to kill a man—I bite my lip and brush my fingers against the cross under my shirt—and that's still the plan, but there is something else going on here. Some reason for this party besides celebrating his early release from prison.

I clench my eyes shut. None of it matters. None of it will matter once Buccero is dead. Cut off the head and the snake dies; that's what Papa always said. That was his advice for bullies at school and pests in the yard.

I caress my gun again, comforted by the grip almost as much as I'm comforted by the warm metal chain against my neck.

I need to find Buccero's room. His study. Go through his things, then hide and wait for his party to be done. Wait for him to come in, stumbling and tipsy. Wait for him to lie down, asleep.

He doesn't need to be awake when I kill him. He doesn't need to know who did it, or why. I have to stop him. That's all this is.

I turn around, and a blade presses to my throat.

A shiver wracks my spine, sending tingles down my limbs. A gasp of air escapes my barely parted lips.

"Damen..." The low, sultry voice of the woman who was once Buccero's head of security, Lydia Escalpo, shoots fear through my limbs.

I thought she was gone.

I should have known she'd return to him when he got out of prison. I should have expected her to be here, but she's been absent from all the press tours. Before, she'd have been glued to his side.

Bright red lips split into a white grin. Her hair is long, dark, and braided against her back. The fingers holding the blade to my throat are decorated with glinting jeweled rings. Her nails are immaculate, painted the same red color of her lips.

Lydia takes a step forward, relaxing her outstretched arm as more of the blade slides along my skin. Her tongue rakes across her top lip.

I shudder. Memories slamming against my mind as I struggle to stay in the present.

Buccero is a sick bastard. A perverted man who enjoys power. When he dies and his soul is dragged into the pits of hell, he won't go as far down as Lydia.

Her spot is reserved at the very bottom, where Lucifer himself can torment her until the end of the universe.

"Damen," she purrs my name again.

She's close. Close enough that I could use my training to take the blade, or at least knock it away. Get enough distance to run. Leave her behind as I sprint to the gate and escape. I tense.

But as she steps to the side, two more figures come out of the shadows behind her. Two guards, guns raised and leveled at my chest. Too far for me to reach before the trigger is pulled.

I swallow. "Lydia." My voice is low, quiet as, below us, the speech ends and the music kicks back up. "I shouldn't be surprised. You always were a loyal dog."

She presses, and I grunt with pain. A warm trickle drips down my neck, the fabric of my shirt absorbing my blood.

"Don't, Damen."

My gut clenches.

"Don't try to be brave. It was foolish to come here." She leans in, inches from my face, and strokes my cheek with a long nail. "You never were very bright."

I'd back away, but the pillar behind me already presses against my back.

"Remove his weapons."

One of the men holsters his gun and moves forward. The other stays away, eyes and muzzle fixed on my chest. I'm relieved of my guns, my blades, even the grappling hook folded up in my pocket. When the man finishes his work, he steps back again.

My pulse thunders through my veins. Each breath comes with a new idea to escape. None of them are halfway decent.

Lydia removes the knife, keeping it in one hand as the other grips my upper arm.

"Move."

I obey, stumbling along as she drags me back the way I came. Down the stairs, the two guards still behind us, still holding their guns to my back, and still too far for me to reach them before they shoot.

"Señora Lydia?"

My heart sinks into my gut. A young man steps into the foyer, a glass of champagne in one hand, and a curious and concerned expression on his face.

It's Arturo, Buccero's new assistant. The one who replaced me. He might be eighteen, but he looks younger. Did I look that young when Miss Belle approached me?

"Nothing to worry about, niño. An intruder, trying to ruin Señor Buccero's beautiful party you put so much work into. I'm taking care of it." She throws him a wink. "No need to tell the boss. I don't want to ruin his night."

My mind scrambles with that tidbit of information. I don't know whether to be relieved or worried that she isn't getting Buccero.

Arturo glances at me, his dark eyes meeting mine for a brief second before he flashes a smile at Lydia and nods. "Of course.

The Señor is lucky to have you back to protect him. We all are." His Spanish is lilting, slower than the coastal tones. I imagine he comes from northern Peru, maybe a village near the Amazon.

Lydia gives a gracious dip of her chin, then tightens her fingers around my arm and yanks me to the front door.

Guilt, shame, and that burning frustration which comes when you've made an irreparable mistake and nothing can fix it, roil in my stomach and chest. My palms are drenched with sweat.

I expect a vehicle. But Lydia doesn't take me toward the cars. Instead, we make for the front gate. Her boots, black leather that stop just below her knees and match the vest over her cream-colored shirt, click against the freshly pressed cobblestone.

"Where are you taking me?" Information. That's what Missa always says. When you are in a hopeless situation, get as much information as you can. The more you know, the more options you have.

"I don't want the Señor getting worked up over a worm like yourself. We are leaving the villa so as to not make a fuss."

Outside the wall of the villa, the world is dark. Stars twinkle in and out of sight, hidden by the rolling clouds. She takes us up the road, toward the bridge I crossed to get here. The gentle rumble of the river is the backdrop to our steps.

Halfway down the road, I have to do something. Lydia could be taking me anywhere. For any purpose. I'm not sticking around to find out.

I close my eyes in a long blink, send up a quick prayer, and spin.

I've cooperated long enough that the change in my behavior startles her. I swoop from her loosened fingers. Grab her wrist. Pull her arm behind her back and put her between me and the guards with the guns.

"Stop," I command. My chest heaves.

Lydia jerks, slashing backward with the blade still in her other hand. I block it, knocking her wrist hard enough that she releases the knife. It clatters to the ground.

In the same movement, she kicks back at my shin. Her heel makes contact and pain flares along my leg.

I swing. My fist connects with the edge of her jaw as she reaches for the fallen knife.

She rolls to the side as a shout breaks the night.

I glance up. The guards are watching Lydia, their guns pointed at me. I heave a breath, straighten, and brush my hair back with my hand.

"No." Lydia curls her lips into a twisted grin. "Don't tell him to stop." She holds up a hand to the guards, her gaze on me. "You want to do this, Damen? You want to test yourself against me?" Her voice is condescendingly sweet.

She looks down at the blade in her hand and tosses it away.

I shift my feet, tensing my core.

"It's been three years, little pup. Have you improved since our last round?"

I bring up my hands, balled into fists, and give her the smallest nod.

My focus is on this moment. This fight. This chance to distract her and the guards, slip down the side of the riverbank, and let the water disguise me and carry me to safety.

Still, the back of my mind wonders what Miss Belle would say about everything that has happened tonight. Her voice flashes through my head. *Hand up. Balls of your feet. Move. Keep moving. Don't be a target.*

I inhale through my nose as Lydia brings her hands up as well. She's got fourteen years on me. Fourteen years, a full decade of mercenary work, and an unhealthy worship-like love for the man I came here to kill.

I don't need to win. I just need to get her down long enough to sprint the twenty yards to the riverbank.

She swings.

I duck to the left, the blow whizzing by my ear.

Her knee connects with my gut.

I curl in, dance back, and take a few shots of my own. The first few miss. She's as fast as I am.

Then I bring in the footwork Missa taught me. A step here. Dancing back. Uneven movements that throw her off until I land a blow against her right cheekbone.

My knuckles sting with pain.

My kick connects too. A shot into her side. Just above her hip bone.

She comes back with a flurry. Blow on blow until there's no dodging, just holding my arms in front of my face. Then she switches in an instant and lands a shot under my elbows into my sternum.

I double over, air gone from my lungs.

As I suck a breath in, her knee flies into my vision and slams against my nose.

I cry out. She doesn't stop. Another blow to the side of the head.

My ears ring. I can't hear. Can't see through the stars dancing in my vision. Can barely breathe through the blood in my nose and my mouth.

I hit the ground. My shoulder cracks on the asphalt and, even blind and deaf, I roll to a crouch.

Laughter breaks through the ringing. Laughter and, as my eyes clear, Lydia's grinning face, blood leaking from her gums, looking down at me.

She spits, a glob of mucus and blood hitting the ground before me.

"Better, little pup. Better, but not enough." She wipes the side of her mouth with a finger and gazes at it thoughtfully. "You might have messed up my lipstick. Rude."

I swallow. The guards have stepped forward to flank her, their weapons still drawn.

"Get up." The laughter in her voice is gone. The joke over. She paces a few yards away and picks up her knife.

I struggle to my feet. She latches her fingers around my arm again and pulls me toward the river.

The bridge is in sight, only a few yards from us now. Pain laces my body. My nose drips blood like a leaky faucet. My ribs ache with each inhale.

Lydia leans closer to me as we near the water. She murmurs in English, her breath hot against my ear. "What was your plan, pup? You want to, what? Fight him? Steal from him?"

I clench my jaw, staring straight ahead through the dark of the night.

"Hmm. Maybe you wanted to come back."

Rumbling sounds in my throat, and I pinch my lips to hold back my words. She doesn't need any more information than she already has. Still, a shudder runs down my spine at the laugh in her voice.

"Did you miss it? The attention?"

My stomach heaves. I meet her gaze for a split second, just long enough to read the amusement in her dark eyes.

We reach the bridge, and Lydia barks for one of the guards to stay at the side, the other to holster his weapon and join us. She tells him to hold me. To not let me jump. She speaks Spanish to them but returns to English as she pulls out her blade again and twirls it around her fingers.

"Didn't you hear, Damen? He doesn't need you anymore." Her smile is all teeth, blood staining her gums bright red. "He has a new toy."

Her finger touches my temple, the nail caressing my skin as she runs it down my face. I struggle against the man holding my arms, trying to block her words. I only need to be loose for a moment. A second of time to jump.

I'll take my chances in the water.

"Did you see him?" Her voice breaks through, even as I try to ignore her words. "He's a cute pup. Younger than you were." She brings the tip of her blade just below my right collar bone.

I inhale and step back. The man behind me forces me forward.

"He screams louder, too," she whispers.

The blade sinks in, and a scream rips from my throat. My vision goes black for a second. My chest heaves as she presses. Slowly. Making me feel every centimeter of metal plunging into my flesh.

I thrash.

The blade slips. Drives up and slashes against my bone.

I swing my head back, my skull connects with the man behind me and the tell-tale crack and yelp suggests I broke his nose.

His fingers loosen. My arms are free. He staggers into my peripheral vision, hands clasped over his face.

Lydia steps forward as I back against the stone carved railing of the bridge. She takes hold of the hilt as I gasp with pain. Twists.

It all goes dark again. Spots of agony interrupt my vision. I lean back.

The edge of the rail is right there. The river rumbles below me. My breath is short. Uneven.

"You shouldn't have come back, little pup," Lydia purrs. She twists again.

I scream again, the sound sinking into a sob. I hunch, bending my knees as though I'm about to collapse.

Lydia scoffs and takes half a step back, making room for my body to hit the ground.

My mind is flooded with pain. I'm going to die. Murdered here. So far from home.

I lean back as Lydia chuckles. Collapse onto the railing.

Enough of me is left to sell it. To make it look real. Look like an accident.

Look like I'm dying.

I roll.

There is no sound now. Just the roaring of wind past my ears as I fall. Fall. Fall. Then a splash. Sinking into dark, cold water. Sinking down. No breath. Only pain.

I can't tell if the darkness is the water, the night, or my mind shutting down. I slip into it as the current pulls me away.

CHAPTER TEN

MISS BELLE

LUNCH AND PANIC

A ita is a lovely restaurant. Clean, quiet—at least at this time of day—and with good food. I sip on my herbal tea; I'm keeping away from caffeine for another week or so. As much as I hate to admit it, my hands are still a bit jittery without the help of coffee. The cup I had the other day did not help my nerves after having a cop in the Manor.

A couple sits at the granite bar, sipping their americanos. Through the window and across the street, children clamber along a vast fenced-in jungle gym. Every movement has my head twitching, making sure I can see everything around me.

The door jingles and, from my place in the far corner, walls to my back, gaze able to sweep every entrance and exit, I watch Emily make her way over to me. Dark hair, cut in a cute, curved bob just above her shoulders, is loose and windswept. The sleeves on her draping purple top are flowy and patched with flowery lace. The edge of the shirt drops almost to her knees. A pair of black polka-dot leggings cover her legs, right up to her little black flats, complete with black bows on the top. Her shirt sleeves barely go past her elbows and my gaze automatically darts to her wrists before I focus back on her face. No bandages. Not even the thick rubber band she started using once we convinced her to go to therapy. A little jolt of joy pumps through my heart.

I stand to meet her, a massive smile on my face, and pull her into a hug. Unlike Missa, she doesn't know about my back or ribs so when she hugs me, her hand presses against my stitches, and she squeezes.

I cover the wince with a cough and take a drink of water before sitting back down.

"Hey, it's great to see you. I'm glad we could get together."

Emily nods, her initial smile slipping just a bit. "Me too. Thanks for making the drive."

"Of course! Anytime I can. I love seeing you." I may be fibbing just a bit here. Not that I don't love seeing my sister, but Nicky and I were always closer. There are definitely times when I could be visiting that I'm binge-watching Firefly instead.

Or Buffy, or anything on the DC app, or reading.

"Me too. Sorry I haven't come to you yet. I can't believe I've lived an hour away for almost three years and still haven't been to your place."

My chuckle is weak, and I quickly shrug off her apologies. I don't want her anywhere near the Manor. Especially not now with cops all over the place.

"If I'm being honest," I lean into the table, giving Em a hard look, "I'd rather have you apologize for giving Mom my number."

She turns pink. "Ahh, Nicky told you about that?"

I've had a week to get over it, but a rush of hot anger makes my fingers twitch. "Yep. And Mom chose a *really* bad time to call."

She looks properly ashamed, and my anger abates. There's no way she could know that our mother would call me in the middle of a tense negotiation with a mercenary.

"I didn't have much of a choice." Em's bottom lip sticks out in a pout. "She threatened to stop paying for classes."

"Don't try that with me." I roll my eyes, but the smile on my lips keeps the mood light. "You know damn well she wouldn't have gotten you kicked out of school just for not giving her my number."

"I am sorry." She grins.

"Well," I grumble. "Next time you could at least give me a heads up."

Her dark eyes sparkle with laughter. "Are you getting a new number?"

I give a lazy wave of my hand. "I think if I got a new one at this point, Mom would hire a P.I. to track me down."

The barely contained laugh breaks through, and Em leans over the table as giggles erupt. I laugh along with her until the waiter arrives to take our order. The food comes. We eat and talk, enjoying each other's company and the delicious meal.

Once I've paid the bill, refusing point blank to let Em chip in even a penny, we grab ice cream cones from a cart parked in front of the playground and walk a few blocks to the gallery displaying her work.

"So." I lick my mint chip slowly, enjoying the cold on my tongue. "What's going on in your world?"

She shrugs one shoulder. "Not really anything. I was hoping you could meet... Well, it doesn't matter." She shakes her head.

"Come on." I give her a light shove. "I barely have time to visit you. Don't hold out on me when we finally get a chance to talk."

She groans. "There's this guy. He comes by every few months from somewhere in Europe. He buys a few pieces of artwork from galleries in the area, then he takes off again. I'm lucky he found the Ramona in the first place. It's not the kind of gallery a guy like him usually checks out." She sighs. "We've kind of hooked up a few times. I like him. Maybe too much. It just doesn't seem like something that'll work for the long term."

Something familiar flickers at the edge of my mind. "Well, if you like him that much I say go for it."

Em shakes her head, her short hair bobbing back and forth just below her ears. "He's not even here right now. He left in a hurry... again."

"People like that, with those kinds of high priority jobs, they don't have the luxury to stay in the same place very long." I suck a chunk of ice cream into my mouth and roll it around, trying to avoid my sensitive front teeth. "He keeps coming back to you; that's good."

"I guess. Even if nothing happens, at least I know he likes my art, right?"

I grin again. We've reached her gallery. Damen is right, she really ought to find a better one. This place feels like someone is running drugs out of it.

Paint peels from the doors, the first A in Ramona needs to be replaced on the window, and the little foyer area is in need of a good sweep.

"Keep me posted. If you guys become official, I want to meet him." I frown, holding open the door as Em passes me. "I don't think I've ever met one of your boyfriends."

"Yeah, you were in L.A. by the time I started college. Freshman year was when I got the first one."

I laugh a little too loudly, and my voice echoes through the building. "I remember him. Mom called me about every three days to complain about him."

She laughs too, a little tinkling laugh that doesn't carry. "That one didn't last very long, thank God."

We move through the front room, a space dedicated to works painted by the owner's family. The little Italian woman who runs the place isn't here at the moment, fortunately for my full stomach as she insists on pumping coffee and butter cookies into me each time I visit.

The paintings here are small. Thin canvas works created by cousins. There are photographs too, black and whites that are special in their simplicity. None of it is the caliber my sister had reached by the time she hit high school.

She leads me through a narrow hall and into the smaller room that holds her works. The prices on the wall aren't nearly what the pieces are worth, but the gallery sets them and it's not something she's ready to argue over.

We start with her new pieces.

Her artwork is stunning. Absolutely stunning. I understand why Damen wants the abstract, even if it's not my favorite style. And after seeing the other one, I'm sure he is the person buying both.

Em has captured Peru. Not the beach fronts, not the city streets, but the mountains. The little village squares, the gorgeous old cathedrals, the wild dogs and cobblestone streets, restaurants, shops, the green of plants everywhere. She's got it all. Rich and deep and textured. It's something one could look at for an hour and still find new details.

I commend her on the paintings and express my wish that she would let me buy one. She tells me again that they both already have a buyer and points out that they're a bit expensive for an author. She's not wrong.

So I find something smaller. A sketch I've been in love with for years. She drew it at a family picnic just before I left for L.A. It perfectly depicts the stream we grew up playing in. The soft burn of nostalgia goes through me as I hand my card to the Italian cousin working the register.

Em blushes and tells me I don't have to get anything. I roll my eyes, making sure she can see me, and tell her I've been wanting this one for years.

We wrap things up, say our goodbyes, and I hop back on my motorcycle—by hop I mean gingerly clamber while moving my ribs as little as possible. My new sketch is tucked into my backpack. Emily hikes her shoulder bag a bit higher and walks to her class. The engine roars to life under me, and I sit straight for a moment, fiddling with my phone.

Damen never did end up calling me back Saturday, and I want to see him while I'm in this part of the city. We need to chat about when he plans on coming back to the Manor.

I tuck in an earbud, stick the business end into my phone, and fasten my helmet in place.

The phone rings as I speed along to his hotel. It rings and rings and goes to voicemail. I frown, the beginnings of concern bubbling in my stomach.

At a stoplight, I pull my phone from my pocket and hold the number one button until speed dial kicks in. Missa answers after the first ring.

"Hey, how'd lunch go?"

"It was nice. Em's doing well. I finally bought that sketch of the creek."

"That's great." She sounds a bit distracted. "Are you headed home?"

"Yeah... I wanted to stop and say hi to Damen, but he's not answering his phone. Have you heard from him in the last couple days?"

"I haven't. Did he call you back on Saturday?"

"No." Something nags at my brain. "Hmm."

"What?"

"I don't know. I just... I wish he'd answer the phone."

"You know how he gets after missions like that last one." Her voice is gentle and soothing as she reminds me that last time Damen was with Prentice, he needed a full month to recoup.

The concern dies down to a simmer in my stomach. Still present, but no more noticeable than usual. I thank her, hang up, and head home, something still nagging at the edge of my brain.

It's still early when I get back to the Manor. I check my email, return a couple messages, and throw on a pair of leggings—with pockets—and a tank top. I sit on the floor to stretch. My room feels empty. Quiet.

I clamber back up, using the bed for support, and make my way downstairs. Josie's nose is buried in *North Tower* by Michelle N. Hagood, the thick red cover obscuring the bottom half of her face. Her eyes make brief contact with mine when I plunk down onto the ornate rug in front of her, then she quickly scans her page to get back to where she was.

I extend my legs, long and slow. Then my arms. Reach up, over my head, and bend forward. Pain pierces my chest. Moving as smoothly as possible, I contort my body through a set of stretches, stopping every time my ribs protest.

When I've loosened up—a little—I pull my headphones and MP3 player from a drawer in the kitchen. Josie lowers the book and raises an eyebrow at me as I move back through the living room toward the front door. I ignore her.

Once my shoes hit concrete I feel better. I start with walking. A steady pace, quick and fluid.

Paramore screams heartbreak in my ears. My mind wanders.

Lacey is doing well with her sister back in California. Delilah's training has officially started; I have some work to do there, but it isn't pressing. Josie doesn't have anything until the end of summer. I should check in with Agent Kalif soon, make sure the feds have their shit together. I still need to talk to Kirskofsky and find out what was worrying him in Poland. He may be a shithead gun runner, but he's also our closest ally in the area.

My muscles itch for a run. My feet send signals up, demanding to pound against the pavement with more force. Once out of sight of the Manor, I relent.

It hurts.

Every step sends a twinge of pain across my chest, but I manage a full block before I stop.

More than last time.

I walk for another few blocks before the residential area crumbles into little storefronts. When I try jogging again, I get a block and a half.

I call Damen again when I get home. Nothing happens. No answer. Just four rings then his voice telling me to leave a message.

I do not.

Instead, I take a deep breath and hop in the shower. After toweling off and changing into jeans and a Wonder Woman T-shirt, I get through the last of the logistical paperwork that needs to be done. There isn't a lot. What with being unable to move around much last week, I got most of my crap done then. The last of my list takes me about an hour. Then I try Damen again.

Voicemail.

Grinding my teeth—I've got to stop before I need a freaking retainer—I leave my room, walk down to the second floor, and knock on Missa's door.

"Yup," comes her soft reply.

Missa chose this room when we found the house. I went for height, my windows looking out over the street and giving me a great view of the block. She went for something on the second floor, but I can't say I blame her.

A bay window takes up most of the wall. It looks out over the back yard with a built-in storage chest that also serves as a seat. Pillows adorn it, matching the thick curtains currently pulled and hooked to the sides. The door past her full-size bed leads to a private bathroom. It's painted to look like a jungle. An array of crawling plants dangle from the windowsill above the bathtub.

Missa sits at the bedroom window, easel up, paint supplies out, working on a really weird, kinda freaky bird skull painting. She hasn't started painting the edges yet, but they have a creepy lace design with crosses and feathers.

Her hair is up in a messy bun; she's switched from pajamas to sweats and a baggy shirt covered in faded paint stains.

"What's up?" Missa glances over at me.

I shake my head. "It's Damen. I'm probably being paranoid, but he still isn't answering. Can you try calling him?"

With a nod, Missa pulls out her phone and makes the call. I hear it from where I've sunk down onto her bed. Voicemail again.

"I'm going to go see him." I stand up. "I don't like that he hasn't called back yet." I shake my head. "There's something wrong."

"He might just still need some time."

"No. Even when he needs time, he knows to at least answer one of us."

She frowns. "That's true." She scratches her nose with the end of her paintbrush.

I rub my hand across my forehead. "I don't like this. After his last mission... blackmail might not have been enough to keep the Vice President from trying for some revenge. I'm going to Damen's hotel."

I turn on my heel.

Missa's voice follows me out into the hallway. "I'll do some digging on this end, see if I can get ahold of him."

I'm at the hotel within the hour. My helmet is barely off my head when I reach the front desk. The small man sitting on a tall stool behind the shelter of the mahogany glances up at me and does a double take. I'm not exactly dressed for the number of stars this hotel boasts.

"I need to ask about a guest. Damen Anderson. He's staying in room 414. It's his regular room; he comes into town every few months."

The man stands, runs a hand through his bushy blonde hair, and heaves a sigh. "I can't confirm who we have staying with us, and I definitely can't give you any information about a guest."

"That's fair." I nod. "Or it would be, if I didn't have the credit card he paid with. We work together, or rather, he works for me."

I pull out the card, as well as my I.D., and he takes them without giving me any trouble. A quick clicking of buttons, some double checking of numbers, and he chuckles.

"All right then. He's scheduled to check out next week and maid service has been declined for the past four days."

"Great. Can I get a key?"

He frowns. "That's not really..."

Before he finishes telling me no, a small handful of twenty-dollar bills land on the counter between us. I don't look at the money. My gaze remains fixed on his face.

He clears his throat. "I, uh... I suppose you are paying for the room." He types another few buttons, and as he slides the room key across the counter, the twenties disappear between his fingers.

"Thanks."

He barely has a chance to respond by the time I'm halfway to the elevator. The metal doors open with a ding, and I step into the metal box. The doors close.

My chest constricts. My skin buzzes. My fingers twitch at my side. I'm not claustrophobic. This is fear for Damen pulsing through me. I repeat this thought a few times, even as the elevator does that thing where you almost feel weightless for a moment, and your stomach tries to practice acrobatics.

A hanging bridge dances before my eyes. Water flows through a ravine beneath my feet, wind roars, the ground sways, and my heartbeat thunders through my ears so loudly, every other sound seems to die away.

Something dings, breaking me out of my frozen terror. The elevator doors open, and I stumble from them onto a classically horrible hotel carpet. My brain is really starting to piss me off. Sure, I'm scared of heights, but I crossed that damn bridge over two weeks ago. I did it. I did it moderately quickly and without any screaming or tears. So why the fuck is it jamming into my head now?

I push the anger aside and force my feet to move me down the hall. Shitty lights blink from dim little fixtures on the walls. 414 looms ahead of me to the right. I remember myself just before I slide the keycard into the lock. Thudding echoes down the hall as I rap my knuckles against the navy-blue paint coating the door.

No answer.

I knock again.

Nothing.

That's enough of that. I slide the keycard in, wait for the click, and pop open the door. A moment of relief hits me once I step into the room. No body. No horrific odor of death or pain. No blood.

No sign, really, that anything is amiss, other than the complete and total lack of signs of life. I live with Damen, and I'm hard pressed to say he's even set foot in this hotel room. No maid service for four days, yet the bed is made, the bathroom is clean and dry, towels hung up, lights turned off; even the TV remote is set nicely in its little place on the bedside table.

I dig a little further. Mini fridge is fully stocked with stupidly expensive snacks and water bottles. Trashcans are empty. Nothing behind the curtains, nothing hiding in the vents. I even check the toilet tank.

I sink down onto the bed next to the helmet I flung down when my search started. I clench my phone, typing in the numbers slowly, afraid of the answers my call might bring me.

"Is he there?" Missa's tone is cold, sharpened against the fear that must be gripping her heart as hard as it grips mine.

"No. I don't think he's been here for at least four days. There's nothing, Missa. No bag, no clothes, no mess, not one clue as to where he could have gone."

I hear her swallow.

"What about your end?" I stand up, grabbing my helmet and leaving the empty room. I make for the stairs this time, as apparently elevators are a problem.

"You need to get home."

A chill goes through me. "What'd you find?" My voice is harsh.

"Maybe nothing. By the time you get here, I'll have more."

"Missa—"

"I've got to go. I'm working on a lead. Get home."

I take the stairs two at a time until my ribs can't take it anymore. I go as fast as I can down the remaining three floors.

The ribs and the slice in my back both share their displeasure as I fling my body over the Ducati and rip away from the curb. My eyes water with the pain, but it is nothing. Nothing compared to my fear for Damen.

If there was ever someone I forced into this business, it's Damen. He didn't want this. He didn't want to leave Peru. He just wanted to do something good for his country, and to do so required a bit more than he was ready to give. So I talked him into it.

Something hisses, and I realize I'm breathing through my teeth. This is the time that having a motorcycle really comes in handy. A patrol car turns on his lights, but by the time he flips a U-turn, I've flown up an onramp and sped between two semis, essentially disappearing into big city traffic.

The hour-long drive takes me forty minutes. There's a good chance I'll be receiving a ticket in the mail from one of those stop light cameras. I don't think it's possible for me to care less.

I chuck the helmet onto the bench and speed-walk through the yard and the kitchen door. My eyes widen at Missa sitting at the kitchen table, laptop open in front of her.

"What'd you find?" I demand.

She looks up at me, fear frozen in her icy blue eyes. Without a word, she pushes the laptop toward me. I tilt the screen and then take a step back, my heart thudding hard against my chest.

Buccero Vincente stares up at me from the screen. A victorious smile on his face, arm raised in the air like he's just won gold for being a class-A piece of shit.

"When?" I say in an exhale.

This is wrong. This wasn't the agreement I made.

Missa hits the spacebar and the video continues. Buccero was released from prison a few months ago. He kept it quiet—the new report says—building up his business and connections before re-entering the business world in Lima.

And enter it he has: a new set of offices, a security team, plans for building in the north, increasing tourism.

A new assistant.

An icy fist clenches around my heart at the sight of the boy by Buccero's side.

I made a promise. When I realized the key to ending the previous president's influence was to take down Buccero, I needed help. He had the president's ear, and the power of a dozen of the wealthiest men in Peru. Not to mention his out-of-country contacts. He was also a recluse. A man who didn't participate in the usual debauchery of the wealthy around him.

Damen though, Damen had his ear. Damen had his attention. And when I found out what he'd been doing to the boy... Damen had a reason to destroy him.

My promise...

My hands are trembling. Fingers shaking as I curl them into fists.

I swore two things when I brought Damen on board. First, I'd protect his family no matter what. Second, Buccero would never see the light of day if we pulled off my plan.

For the last three years, I thought I'd kept it. His family has been safe. And Buccero has been rotting in prison. He was supposed to be rotting for 20-25 years.

"How wide was this broadcast?"

"International news."

I close my eyes. A chill runs down my spine. "Fuck." I rub a hand across my face, scratching at the side of my mouth. After a moment, my gaze meets Missa's again.

She nods. "He's there."

Pulling the laptop toward her again, she switches tabs and gestures for me to sit. I stand behind her chair instead.

"Card statements?"

"Yeah. He booked a flight for Sunday morning. The first one out."

"Shit." I step to the side, lean forward, and brace myself against the table, breathing hard. My head feels dizzy. I need to slow my breaths. "It's Tuesday. He's been there... a full forty-eight hours?"

Missa says nothing.

"Why hasn't he contacted us? Why didn't he tell us he was leaving?" My voice grows louder, angrier. I slam my fist down on the table, immediately regretting it as pain blossoms up the edge of my hand and through my pinky.

"The next flight leaves in four hours. We should leave here within thirty minutes. It lands tomorrow morning at 9am. I'd prefer to get there sooner, but there's not much to be done about it now."

My mind is still thudding with frustration, so it takes me a moment to catch her words. "We?"

Missa doesn't respond right away. She closes her laptop and scoots out her chair, standing up to face me. "Yes. We.

You handled Lacey's thing in Thailand by yourself; that's not happening again."

My thoughts flash away from the conversation, going through a flood of images. The weight of a blade in my hand, the feeling of steel through bone... the scent of the burn that comes right after you fire a gun. The sound of a flash grenade.

Pain splinters across my chest and back as I breathe deeper.

Fear strikes my heart.

"No."

Missa gives me a look that is all too familiar. It's the same expression I wear when someone tries to tell me what to do, or what not to do. Eyebrow raised, eyes wide, hands on hips, she looks an odd combination of ready to laugh and ready to slap me.

"No? Try again. You may run the rest of this house, but you don't run me, and you know it." Her tone is not level; not this time. It's dark and dangerous and makes me shiver in spite of myself.

My left hand rubs across my lips in a subconscious movement. I touch the little divot on my forehead, pressing until sharp pain stabs across my eyes. "I don't think it's a good idea for us both to be gone from the Manor. Especially not right now. We've got plenty here that needs attention."

Missa's eyes glint, and I actually take a step back, running into the counter behind me. I lean, trying to look casual and not as though I'm contemplating how easily she could kick my ass right now.

Don't get me wrong, we're pretty damn matched most of the time. If anything, I'm stronger than she is, due to her slender build and graceful frame. But I'm still nursing my injuries. And she's got a scary look in her eye.

"If anyone should stay in New York, it's you."

I let out a humorless chuckle. "I'm the one who got Damen into this mess. I'm not about to sit at home and let you take care of it."

"Oh, you mean like I did with Lacey?"

The hurt and frustration in her voice confuses me. "What? No. You didn't cause her issues with Nathan. You aren't the reason she took the mission."

She tilts her head and squints at me. "You think the Guides accept missions just for you? You think I'm not part of what pushes our girls to take on the jobs they do? The risks?"

I exhale loudly. "It's different. I can't stay here while Damen's in danger."

The muscles in Missa's jaw clench as her hands do the same. "And you think I can?"

My head pounds. We shouldn't be doing this now. There is too much to do before the flight leaves, too many variables we should be considering rather than having this fight.

"How long do you think we'll be gone?"

A brief flash of surprise flickers across Missa's face, and I know she was expecting more of a fight. It feels like one has been building between us for a while now. Since I got back from Thailand, and maybe before that. Maybe it's been coming on for a long time, and I've been too blind to notice.

The thought leaves a sad pit in my chest.

"A few days. Maybe a week." Missa turns back to the table, casting me a sidelong glance as she opens the laptop. "There's the flight out and back, two full days. Then, however long it takes to find Damen. If he flew out because he's worried about his family, that's where he'll be headed. If..." she sighs. "If he's there for something else, it might be more difficult."

I nod.

"Get the tickets. And get us checked in. I'll talk to the girls and make a few calls to our contacts down there."

Missa catches my gaze and holds it for a second before returning the nod.

The tension is still there. It pulls on me as I leave the room; but there's nothing I can do about it right now. We've got bigger fish and all.

Alex and Sarah aren't in their rooms. I find both women sitting in the backyard. Alex is reading *You Can't Touch My Hair: And Other Things I Still Have To Explain* by Phoebe Robinson, and Sarah's flipping through a cookbook with dazzling pictures that make my mouth water. A small Bluetooth speaker hums Whitney Houston.

I almost feel bad for interrupting their relaxing afternoon.

They both cast a glance at me when I open the door. Alex goes back to her book, but Sarah frowns and closes hers.

"What is it?"

"It's time to gear up ladies. We've got trouble."

Chapter Eleven

Miss Belle

People Who Know You

Missa and I have been together since before I can remember. She was there in elementary school, middle school, high school, and the first two years of college. The longest we've ever been apart was the beginning of Junior year of college when she transferred to UCLA and disappeared for six months.

I followed her not long after things deteriorated with Don and... well, the rest is history. The point is, she's always been there for me. Even when I don't want her to be.

Like now, for instance.

I feel her eyes on me, her gaze lingering on my face as the TSA guy pats down my waist through my heavy sweatshirt. I feel her watching me as I sit at the gate, waiting to board our flight to Bogota.

We have an hour-long layover in El Dorado Luis Carlos Galan Sarmiento International Airport—come on people, let's try for shorter names, please—before we get to Peru. Then we try to find Damen.

He was in Lima last we checked. We know which I.D. he's using, because he used the credit card that goes with it at the hostel he's hopefully still staying at.

I fidget with the strap of my go-bag. I emptied it out, washed all the clothes, and re-filled it after Thailand. It's been a long while since I've needed to use it twice in such a short amount of time.

Once upon a time, Missa and I handled pretty much every mission. Even when we had guides doing the hard part, we were somewhere nearby, ready to help. But with so many girls (and boys) now, it's harder to be everywhere at once. Fortunately, with Erin running the start of the training program, and plenty of women on our team who've been with us for years, we don't often need to jet across the world to problem-solve.

I check my phone. No missed calls. No messages. No nothing.

We've given up on calling. There are enough notifications on his phone. He should have called us.

He shouldn't have left the country without telling us. But even doing such a stupid and dangerous thing... After seeing so many missed calls, texts, and voicemails (we filled his inbox), he should have called us back by now.

Which means something is wrong.

Missa called his mother's house before we left the Manor. They haven't heard from him. If he's going home, he should be getting there soon. Hopefully we'll hear something when we land.

If something *isn't* wrong, it's going to be once I find him.

They call the first boarding group, and I jump at the noise. My neck itches at the sound of people standing, shuffling, moving around me as I sit still. Or try to. My leg pumps up and down against the ground in a jittery rhythm.

When it's our turn, I'm up from my seat faster than Missa. The thought of sitting on a plane, cooped up for almost twelve hours (not including the layover) is petrifying. But I can't let her see that. She'll insist on a visit to Doc.

Though, as someone a few gates away drops a metal water bottle and the resounding sound feels as though it is pounding into my brain with violent fury, I grudgingly think she may be right.

Ugh. There's nothing worse than someone else being right.

We are the last people on the plane, one of the detriments of buying tickets so late. Still, I don't mind not having people behind me. I step over the small gap of air between plane and dock, and they shut the door behind me. I focus on my breaths, in and out, as I am sealed into an airtight cylindrical container full of strangers.

Flying is hard. Even for the regular flier, someone in business who boards planes weekly, it gets rough. The tight spaces, stale air, weird-tasting water, is a lot.

Find a way to make yourself comfortable—besides taking off your shoes. Get a neck pillow, noise-canceling headphones, a blanket for when your seat neighbor blasts the air. Stretch before you get on the plane, and don't worry about anyone looking at you funny, you're all in the airport and may as well try to survive the flight as best you can.

If you have trouble sleeping on planes, bring calming music, a boring book, something to fidget with. There are lots of ways to get past the anxiety that builds when flying. Find yours and stick to it. An easy journey will make the trip all the better.

Chapter Twelve
Damen
Am I Dead?

I don't think I'm dead. I'm cold, for starters. Also, as consciousness returns, so does feeling. Water, lapping against my torso. Mud, thick and grainy against my chin. Pain, every inch of my body in pain. The worst of it is just below my right shoulder.

Everything is dark.

I lift my left hand, grateful it works, and reach across to gently prod the source of the agony. My fingers brush against the hilt of a knife, and a splintering shock shoots through me. I gasp, roll—worse, bad idea—and lay moaning and huffing on the ground for a long moment.

Moonlight peeks between the trees as wind blows the branches this way and that.

I don't know how long I lay there. Staring up, watching the moon move across the midnight blue sky.

It's Em that gets me up. The thought of her waiting on my promised messages finally pulls me to my feet. Then the thought of Miss Belle finding my body, delivering the news to my family, that gets me up the steep riverbank.

I come out on the road. I can't be too far from my car, not with the wealthy homes still in view across the asphalt from me. I trudge upriver, feet dragging against the gravel, limbs pulling me to the earth with unwavering weight.

I'm going the right way. Right? The car has to be here. Somewhere.

Racking coughs break from my lungs. I duck into the vegetation, trying to muffle the sounds. Each burst slams my head with pain. My shoulder more so. My knees collide with the ground. Another shudder of pain.

"*Damen.*"

Wide-eyed, I swallow down my next cough. Fear grips my chest as Em's voice fills my ears. I glance around.

There is no one. Nothing around me but thick leaves, dark sky, and asphalt that smells like rain.

She knew...

She knew where I was going. Knew it was Peru. What if she...

I pull myself to my feet. Vines rip in my hands as I use them to lift myself up. My mouth is dry, tongue cottony and tastes like cardboard.

I check one more time. A glance in every direction to make sure she's not really here. Then I stumble along. Continue down the road at an agonizingly slow pace. Time passes. Eventually, as I round a shallow bend, my little car comes into sight. Snug against the roadside where I left it.

With gasping breaths, I duck alongside a wheel well and pull a key from the magnet I planted there. I crawl into the driver's seat, dirtying everything I touch with mud and blood.

As I heave the door shut, a figure appears in the passenger seat. I jerk back, blinking furiously.

My words come out ragged. "You're not here, right?"

Em's lock of dark hair brushes past her shoulder as she turns to look at me. She flashes a smile, the rare one that shows her teeth. She's only used it a few times with me. Residual nerves from being bullied about braces as a kid keep her smile tight.

The hilt of the blade in my shoulder catches my attention in my peripheral vision.

"Don't pull that out."

My throat locks up as she speaks with Miss Belle's voice. Tears build in my eyes. I nod. Her hand reaches toward me. It's Em's hand. I know that. I know her fingers, perpetually stained with paint, or charcoal, or ink. But it's Miss Belle's voice again as Em's hand touches my cheek.

"... somewhere safe."

"What?" I whisper. I run the back of my hand under my nose. Tears dribble down my cheeks.

Em brushes one away with her thumb.

The words are muffled. Distant and distorted and not clear in my waterlogged ears.

"...away from the scene. They might search the river. Make sure you're...."

As the voice fades, Em fades.

"No." It comes out as a plea. "Em, don't..."

I'm talking to a dull gray passenger seat. Em is gone. Miss Belle's voice is gone.

Somewhere safe. I have to get somewhere safe.

It's a haze as I drive. A miracle I don't kill myself. Each set of passing headlights blinds me. Pain pulses at my head. I've left the knife in, but blood still pools in my seat, dripping from my chest. It would soak my clothes if I weren't already drenched.

Twenty minutes in, the shivers start. My teeth chatter together like one of those horrible toys Em likes to play with at Halloween stores.

I'm so cold.

I take a left. The headlights bounce up and down as the car rumbles down a dirt road. Pocketed with rocks and holes, small drives leading to clean and comfortable homes.

I grew up on a road like this.

I'm going too fast. This becomes clear as the house looms ahead. Pale blue shutters, creamy stucco walls, dark windows. They're asleep.

I slam the breaks and jerk the wheel. The car careens to the side. The back bumper hits something.

My head knocks against the side window as I come to a halt.

The headlights shine onto the front porch. The door opens.

My vision goes as figures hurry down the wooden steps. Voices pull me, but I'm lost. Lost and in pain and fading.

The door wrenches open, and I slump to the side. Everything goes black.

Chapter Thirteen
Miss Belle
Each Breath Stings

My phone is out the second our wheels hit the tarmac.

The flight was... unfortunate. My back is a wrecked knot of twisted muscles and tension. Same in my neck. My chest, the bruised ribs which have been slowly healing, did not enjoy twelve hours of sitting and laying on airport chairs.

Each breath stings.

No calls. No messages.

My fingers go white around the phone, my arm trembling.

Missa's fingers touch my shoulder. I jerk, heaving a sigh as she gestures for us to follow the other passengers. I'm holding up the line to get off the plane.

How long was I staring at my phone?

I rise, grip the handle of my bag, and keep pace behind her through the airport. Geometric designs pass me by as I stare ahead. Massive glass windows make up the wall of the entrance; they're stunning and blinding.

We step out of the sliding doors into Lima, Peru.

She's a beautiful city. One of my favorites. One of the few places I'd traveled to before all the Miss Belle stuff started. My family came here one summer when I was in high school.

Nostalgia hits.

Visiting Em was good. Necessary. My mind drifts to my little brother...

"Belle?"

I shake my head and focus on Missa. She's at the door to a cab, her expression concerned beyond the norm. I suck a bit of my lip between my teeth and bite down until I'm back in this space with my whole consciousness. Blood pools on my tongue.

I smile and nod, climbing into the back and resting my go-bag on the ground between my feet. Missa gives me a look as she climbs in as well. Then she gets to business, leaning forward and giving the cabbie the rest of the directions. He tries to overcharge. She snaps back in perfect Spanish, but he takes in her blue eyes, golden hair, and pale skin.

Try as she might, the accent will never sound like native Peruvian. They agree on a number that's higher than the average, but less than what he originally asked for. I don't know why she bothered. As she leans back against the seat with a disgruntled expression, I raise an eyebrow.

"Why not just pay him and be done with it?" I ask in English. "We have the money for it."

Missa meets my gaze. Something sparks in those blue eyes. A flash of anger or worry or something else in that wheelhouse of emotion that I can't name. She doesn't respond.

As the cab pulls away from the curb, dives headlong into traffic, and zips us into the central district of Lima, she is quiet. Morning traffic turns the thirty-five minute journey into closer to an hour. My knee bounces up and down, up and down. My sight goes blurry as I stare out the window, watching the cars pass too close to us, the buses full of people.

Finally, twenty minutes in, I break the silence.

"Backpackers hostel?"

Missa glances at me. "Yes. And a breakfast yesterday morning in Miraflores District. Then he rented a car."

I frown. Yes, I already knew this, but it helps to think out loud. And I was about to explode from the quiet. "Do you think he's left the city?"

Missa shrugs. Her sweater, a pale creamy thing bought at a crochet stand at an art festival, hangs off her slender shoulder. "I don't understand why he would. Well." She grimaces. "I don't understand why he'd come here in the first place. Let alone without telling us."

I nod, but my agreement is about him not telling us. Not about his reason. I have a feeling I know why he's here. It's a gnawing in my gut that's been going since I saw that news clip about Buccero's release.

Thirty seconds later, my suspicion is confirmed.

My phone goes off. I flip it open, feel a flutter of disappointment that it's not Damen's name on the screen, and then a rush as the words *Peru Confidential* register. With half a grin, I put the phone to my ear.

"Señora Luccela, an honor to receive a call from you. I trust everything is well with your family?"

A code phrase, designed to let me know if someone found her. Found out she works for me. Has her hostage.

My eyes go wide as a strange man's voice responds.

"Who is this? *Abuela,* when are you going to tell me what's going on?"

"Hush, *niño.*" Luccela's unmistakable gravelly voice comes through the line. There's a pause, some jumbled shushing, and then her tone fills my ear. "Señorita Belle, how are you doing?"

"I'm well. How are you?" I stifle a chuckle as Missa raises an eyebrow at me. Luccela didn't respond with the phrase that would mean she's in danger, so amusement rather than worry is at the forefront of my mind.

"Old, Señorita. I'm old. So old, in fact, that my grandson feels the need to help me with every little thing. Including *dialing the phone*," she snaps.

In the background, I hear, "You were complaining that you couldn't read the numbers, *Abuela*."

"It was a joke! A joke. I'm funny, Caleb. *Dios.*"

"Señora," I interject, a smile crawling across my lips, "what can I do for you?"

"I want to know when I'll be getting my guns back."

The smile freezes. A chill runs through my whole body, hairs standing on end as my gaze slowly turns to Missa.

"What guns, Señora?"

The banging of pots and pans sound on her end of the phone. Water pours, a cupboard closes. "The guns you had borrowed on Monday. I forgot to ask your man when and where I should collect them. Will he be able to bring them back? Or should I prepare Caleb for a journey."

"*Que?*" comes her grandson's voice again.

"Don't eavesdrop, Caleb," Luccela barks.

I'm numb. Numb and frozen for a few long seconds. A car slides too close to us and the cabbie lays on the horn.

I twitch into focus. "Señora, I'm sure Damen will have your things returned soon. Would you be able to remind me how much he borrowed? So I may wire you the correct amount? In fact, I am in the country as we speak, going to help him with his assignment. I will ensure you don't have to drive far, if at all."

"Excellent. I can always count on you, Señorita Belle. I will have Caleb email you the information. It was lovely to hear your voice. Come for lunch if you can while you're here."

I nod absently. "That sounds lovely, Señora. *Gracias.*"

The phone clicks. My cell drops from my trembling hand and lands in my lap. Missa puts a hand on my arm.

"What was that?"

I swallow and look at her. The fear I've been pushing down since we learned of Damen's return to Peru comes rising up like a tidal wave. "Damen. He went to Señora Luccela's. He has an arsenal."

"Shit," Missa breathes. "Should we go straight to the office building?"

I shake my head, uncertainty clawing at me. "I don't... No. Let's hit the hostel first, see if we can find him there, or at least learn something about his plan. If we come up blank, we can split up. I'll go to the offices, and you can wait for him at the hostel."

Missa glares at me. "Or we leave a note at the hostel and go to the offices together."

My lip curls, but I can't argue with her. Not because I don't want to, but because it'll start a whole spiel about how I need to talk to Doc and I shouldn't be alone and blah blah blah.

"Belle?"

"Yeah." I snap back with a nod. "Hostel first. Offices if we can't find out where he went next."

"We'll have wifi at the hostel. I'll be able to pull up his card report. See if he paid for anything nearby."

Another nod. We fall back into silence. This time strained and tense as we both imagine the worst of what might be happening to Damen. At least, that's what my mind is doing.

Even as I force myself to remember his year of training. To remember that he spent time with Erin in Chicago. He was in Alaska for a month, Mexico for two, and flitted across Europe for four.

He knows how to fight. Knows how to shoot. Knows...

Fuck.

He knows not to go off on his own, damnit.

I glare out the window as the cab slows at the curb and the driver gives us a smile in the rearview. Missa returns it. I exit the car, snatch my bag, and stride toward the door to the hostel without another word.

Missa catches up by the time the person at reception buzzes the lock and lets us through. We climb the marble stairs, and Missa checks us in while I wander through the lobby. The area is small but comfy. Couches, a couple of computers, and two double doors open into the bar. There's no one serving alcohol at the moment—it's eleven in the morning after all—but a few people sit at little tables against the windows, sipping on tea and finishing off what looks like strawberry jam spread across biscuits.

My stomach grumbles. We sped out of the airport, and I haven't eaten since last night.

"Anything?" I murmur as Missa comes up beside me.

She hitches her bag across her shoulder and shakes her head. "They wouldn't confirm or deny him checking in."

I give half a shrug as my gaze sticks on the field across the street outside the window. We're very near a beautiful museum, and the vibrant green grass extending from its side wall fills most of the block giving tourists a nice place to lay out a blanket and picnic.

"Do you want to stay here? I got us a room. We can drop our bags and make for the office building."

I shake my head and rip my gaze from the window. "Let's get some work done first. You hit the bank info, and I'll put another call in to Carmen. See if she's heard from her brother. I know Damen had a few contacts in the city, but that was three years ago. He shouldn't still be in touch with anyone. If he has been..."

She nods. "To the room then?"

"Yeah."

Half an hour later I bite into a blueberry muffin Missa picked up down the street just as my phone rings. I chew, my eyes narrowed as a surge of frustration runs through my gut.

Chew, chew, chew... It's a Peru number. I swallow—painfully.

I pick up, nerves in my stomach. "Hello?"

"Miss Belle?"

I frown. "Maria?" Damen's mother.

"*Si,*" she goes on in Spanish, "Damen is here, Señora Belle. He is hurt. Do we need to leave? Can we take him to the hospital?"

A shudder wracks my body. I look to Missa, currently bent over her laptop with the edge of her thumbnail between her teeth. She meets my gaze. In an instant she's straightened, closed the computer, and is shoving things into her bag.

"No hospital," I murmur. I clear my throat and pour some damn strength into my voice. Though every limb feels weak. "How hurt is he?"

"We stopped the bleeding. He said not to call, but—"

"Mama?" A shrill voice sounds on her end of the phone. Similar to Damen's tone, but an octave higher. His twin. Carmen.

"Don't give me that look, *mija*. I had to tell her. He is hurt." Maria's muffled voice becomes clear again. "You know where we are, yes? Are we in danger? Do we need to leave again?"

I lick my lips. "Can you put Damen on?"

"*Lo siento, Señora,* he is sleeping still. He's barely woken since he arrived. He was stabbed in the shoulder. He's been beaten."

"I'm in country." I close my eyes and suck in a deep breath, holding the air in my lungs until it aches before I release. "I can be there in a few hours. Sit tight—don't leave the house. If—when he wakes up, find out if anyone followed him. If they did, go to the safe-house. But for now, don't move him."

"*Si.*"

"Keep him alive, Maria."

Her tone goes cold. "That is what you were supposed to be doing."

There is a click, and then the dial tone.

My left hand closes around the phone. My right trembles so hard I have to jam it under my thigh to stem the movement.

"Arequipa?" Missa murmurs behind me.

I nod. A few seconds pass, and then I'm on my feet. I didn't unpack my bag, so it doesn't take more than a moment to pull my shoes back on, wrap my muffin in a napkin for later, and head to the door.

"He'd better be alive when we get there," I mutter under my breath.

Missa nods. Her hand finds mine. Our fingers interlace and we hurry through the lobby, down the marble stairs, and hail a cab back to the airport.

Chapter Fourteen

Damen

Hard Truths

I wake in a strange room on a familiar couch. It's an odd feeling, accompanied immediately by pain which drives all other thought from my mind. I reach up, grasping for the railroad spike that must be plunging into my shoulder.

Instead, I find gauze. Bandaging over my bare chest. My fingers come back red.

I'd go to wipe them on the blanket covering the lower half of my body, but I recognize the weave. The pattern. The soft alpaca wool used to create it.

I sit up.

Another burst of pain. This time from my head as the room spins. I gaze around, jaw gaping as realization hits.

The couch I am on presses against a wall; across from me is a small television, currently dark. A fireplace and mantle are on the right-hand wall. Another couch, smaller, sits across from the fire and, between the two couches, is an old wooden rocking chair.

There are little scratches on the arms, from where my sisters and I picked at the wood when Mama rocked and sang us to sleep.

A framed picture sits on the mantle.

Without thinking, I stand. The pain is dim in the back of my head as I cross the carpeted floor and stare, unblinking.

Rosie had just been born. Her little fingers grasp my father's thumb. His other hand ruffles Carmen's head. She has her arm looped around his leg. He and Mama are snuggled on the couch, baby in her arms, Carmen beside my father, and me on the floor between them. Mama's hand is on my shoulder.

I scan the image, tears forming in my eyes, before my vision is stuck on Papa. On the smile that mine looks so much like. On the love in his eyes as he gazes at Mama, even though she'd just demanded he look at the camera for once.

"At least you can stand."

I wheel around hard enough that my injured body can't quite keep up with my head. I tip sideways as everything spins again.

Carmen rushes forward and catches me.

I yelp. Her hands shift from the bandaged shoulder where she caught me. She holds my left side and moves with me back to the couch.

I sink onto the cushions and stare at my sister. She looks the same as she did three years ago. Her jet-black hair is long. The braid is a day old, strands of hair falling around her face and obscuring the multiple piercings on both ears. She has a few new ones.

Her dark eyes, a perfect match for mine, are alert and careful. The physical pain feels like nothing compared to the ache in my heart at seeing her again.

A few seconds pass in stiff silence. Then I ask, "What... what happened?"

She raises an eyebrow and settles next to me. Leaning forward, forearms resting on her knees, she picks at a bracelet around her wrist. "What do you remember?"

I swallow. How much to say... about Buccero, my attempt on his life, my being in the country without telling them?

The silence grows too long, and she curls her lip, throwing me a dirty look. "He's out. That's why you're in Peru. I'm not stupid, Damen. I follow the news."

"Does Mama know?"

She shakes her head. "I don't want to move again. We just got settled here. She has her church group twice a week and..." She exhales half a chuckle. "Rosie's cat is pregnant."

"I tried to..." I glance around. The living room has a hall leading deeper into the house, and a half-wall where someone in the kitchen might socialize with visitors. My little sister and mother are nowhere to be seen.

"They're out back. Collecting eggs and feeding the chickens. And Rosie is checking on Whiskers."

I bob my head, trying to focus on which details to tell Carmen, but I'm struck by the fact that I didn't know Rosie has a cat named Whiskers. A shot of regret aches in my chest.

"I came to kill him."

Carmen nods. She shifts, pulling one knee up onto the couch to face me, a serious furrow in her brow. "Did you? Did you finish it?"

Lydia's face swims to the front of my mind. A sneer wrinkles my nose. Another ounce of pain as a cut I hadn't noticed splits on my top lip.

"No. His head of security—"

"Lydia," Carmen growls through gritted teeth.

I nod. "She caught me. Did this," I gesture to my bandaged shoulder, "before I escaped."

"Does she..." Carmen's eyes widen in alarm. "Does she know where you are?"

I shake my head.

"Damen," her voice holds a warning, "you were half-unconscious when you rammed into my car last night."

I wince.

"How do you *know* she didn't follow you?"

I swallow and run through the events of last night. "I fell. I tipped off a bridge and into a river. There was no one around when I came to, and no one in sight when I managed to get back to my car."

Carmen lets out a breath. She nods. "All right then. So," she stands and paces a shallow circle in the living room, "what's the plan?"

I frown up at her.

"You failed on your own. Obviously, you need help. How do we finish the job? How do we kill Buccero?"

Mama comes in not long after that, and I'm forced back to the couch. The papers Carmen and I had been fiddling with, a rough sketch of Buccero's villa and the numbers of guards I spotted, remain on the kitchen table.

"*Mijo,*" Mama murmurs, settling on the couch beside me. "What is going on?"

I swallow and glance at Carmen as a shiver runs down my spine. This wasn't... I never...

My sister gives me a hard look then nods.

She and Rosie know. I told Carmen everything Buccero had done—and was still doing—to me the night Miss Belle first contacted me. Rosie figured it out on her own, though I suspect Carmen gave her some hints. But Mama? No.

I didn't explain to her why I stopped working for Buccero. Not truthfully. It was enough for her to know that he was corrupt. That he was using his position as the right hand to the president to sell off huge chunks of native land in northern Peru. That he was hurting our country, our father's people.

I don't think that will be enough to explain me trying to murder him. Not for the woman clutching the crucifix around her neck like a lifeline.

"Buccero is free from prison, Mama," Carmen says in Spanish as she sinks into the rocking chair.

From the kitchen, Rosie appears with a cup of hot chocolate for me. She hands it over, then curls up like a cat on the big couch, her feet tucked under her, a steaming mug of her own drink between her fingers.

Mama lifts the cross to her lips and murmurs under her breath for a few seconds.

Carmen scoffs.

Rosie looks at me. Her dark eyes, identical in shape and color to our mother's, meet mine. She's changed the most in the time I've been gone. But she's still only eighteen. A child. The same age I was when I got the job in the capital.

Yet she is older than I was. The death of our father at such a young age, me and Carmen involved in our own lives, Mama trying to support us... she had to grow up faster than we did.

Now, according to the last phone call I had with Mama before everything went wrong, she's been accepted into a nursing school in Arequipa.

She's growing into the young woman our father hoped she'd be.

Rosie furrows her brow, an unspoken question in the tilt of her head. I think I know what she's asking. I nod.

She swallows and returns the gesture. "What are you going to do now?" she murmurs.

Mama looks up, finished with her prayer, and glances from Rosie to me. "What do you mean, 'do now?'"

Rosie doesn't look at our mother. "Buccero can't be allowed in the world, Mama. He has to be stopped."

Carmen nods, halting her rocking and leaning forward. "Rosie is right. We can finish this. Take him out."

"*What?*"

I purse my lips and give Carmen a meaningful glare.

She ignores me. "Why do you think Damen is here, Mama? To drag Buccero back to jail? The man has to be stopped. Permanently."

The burn from Mama's gaze sizzles my skin. "You came here to kill a man? *Damen*! That is not how I raised you. You are a good boy. A good man. You do not kill."

I stay silent. The pain in my shoulder has started up again, the meds worn off through the morning. She's right. I haven't killed before. It shouldn't be a source of shame, and certainly no one in the Guides makes it feel that way, but still... I'm one of only a couple of us who have yet to pull the trigger on someone.

I thought I was happy with it. I even told Miss Belle from the start, I want to avoid killing if at all possible. I wanted to keep my hands clean of that sin.

"Fine." Carmen heaves a sigh and stands. "If you won't let *precious* Damen do it, I'll kill him."

Mama stands as well, fury in her gaze. "You will *not.* I will not allow my children to damn themselves to hell over a corrupt politician."

Carmen responds, her voice rising as she shouts about Mama not understanding. About her being blind because of her religion.

Rosie stares at me. Always the calmest of us. The steadiest. Tears pearl at the corners of her eyes.

My head aches. My heart hurts. Everything hurts.

"Mama," I mutter.

She doesn't hear me. Now she is shouting, telling Carmen she spends too much time away from home. Takes too many risks in the mountains. This has turned from an argument about me and devolved into a debate that has clearly happened many times before.

Carmen never wanted to be home this long. She wanted to get out. Live her own life.

It's because of me she hasn't been able to.

"Mama," I say again, louder this time.

She stops and turns to me. Carmen glances my way as well, cheeks flushed and breathing heavy.

"I need to tell you..." I falter, shame carving a hole in my gut.

Carmen shakes her head. "Damen, you don't have to. It's fine." She cuts the air with her hand, and I know what she means. She'll take the heat from our mother. Like she always has. Protecting my secrets since we were fourteen, and I realized I liked looking at boys the same way I looked at girls.

Meanwhile, I let her take every ounce of criticism Mama throws at her.

"I need to tell you the truth." My eyes burn. I run a hand along my jaw and wince as I find bruises leftover from Lydia's fists.

Mama has lost the heat in her cheeks. She sinks onto the couch and takes my hand in hers. "Of course, *Mijo*."

I glance at Carmen, unsure if I want her there. If I want to leach from her endless store of strength, or get her and Rosie out of the room before I let slip everything that has happened in the last four years to our mother. Well, the parts of it involving Buccero at least.

Carmen waits. After a few agonizing seconds, I jerk my head toward the hallway.

She goes to Rosie, touching our little sister's shoulder and leading the two of them out of the room.

I fish my own cross from under my shirt and rub my fingers along the metal. Then I tell my mother the truth about my job as Buccero's assistant, and the real reason I left Peru three years ago.

Traveling is an adventure. Cut it however you like, from a trek to the bookstore to a flight around the globe, anything can be a quest, adventure, journey, what-have-you. It's important on those farther flung trips to give information to the people who care about you. When you're city-hopping, take that extra few minutes to call a friend and let them know where you're going. This is especially important when traveling alone. Keep people updated on your location—but for the love of all things do NOT post your location on social media. Save those fancy pictures of a specific locale for after you've left it.

Chapter Fifteen

Miss Belle

This Is Why I Don't Go Home For Christmas

Say what you will, but I'm a big fan of keeping secrets from my parents. Plenty of reasons why... and you can probably guess most of them. I like having my life private. Also the whole spy-ring thing.

Missa is driving. Again. I offered this time. I like being behind the wheel. I know it's shocking but having control over the vehicle I'm in is important to me. I don't need Doc to explain why. It's pretty obvious.

We managed to find a flight pretty quickly. Peru has a decent amount of tourism and while most of them head to Cuzco for Machu Picchu, Arequipa has its fair share of beautiful sights for visitors.

The airport car rental place was crowded. Probably why Missa insisted on driving. We got halfway through the rental process when I had to step outside for some deep breaths.

Damen's mom lives in what you could call the suburbs. Not quite the sidewalks and lawns we have in the States, but the collections of houses, small yards, and winding roads are similar in their own way.

I finished my muffin a while ago, and my stomach rumbles its discomfort as we make a sharp left. Missa turns down the music as we get close.

The dirt road leading to Maria's house is busy. We slow to a stop as a gaggle of chickens—gaggle? Is that geese? What are chickens? Anyway—cross the street. A man walks along behind them, a large thin stick thwacking the ground on either side of the feathered creatures to keep them going straight.

The house is at the end of the street and a rush of relief hits me as I see it.

I bought it. Planned the move when rumblings reached me that a few of Buccero's ex-contacts were moving through the village Damen's family had been in before. But I hadn't seen the place in person.

The home is tiny. Maria insisted upon it. A little yard in the back with some chickens, a goat, and... I think she said a cat? Animals. There is room for animals.

The walls are pale blue, light shutters on the windows are closed. Carmen's car, a small, old dark green thing, has a massive dent in the left side. It goes across both doors.

Beside it, a second car is parked and covered with a large tarp.

"Damen's?" Missa asks as we pull up beside the tarped car.

"Probably. Be ready in case it's not."

She nods and untucks a small gun from her boot. I click open the glove compartment and take out a significantly larger weapon. With a glance toward the road—the chicken herd is gone, and the street is deserted—I climb out of the car, silently move up the steps of the wooden porch, and position myself beside the front door.

I knock.

Missa steps up as well, her back to the wall on the opposite side of the door.

The house is silent for a long moment. I lean my ear to the wall and catch the sound of scuffling, hushed voices, and then footsteps.

I pull away, gun held firm in my hands, safety off, trigger finger resting along the muzzle. Heat rushes through my limbs. My heartbeat thunders through my ears.

Carmen opens the door a crack and gives me a quick full-body scan. She raises an eyebrow, sticks her head around the door, catches sight of Missa, and gestures for both of us to enter the house.

We enter a small living room. To the right is a dining nook and kitchen with a low wall separating it from a narrow hall leading further into the house. The fireplace is empty save some ash. Twin couches rest against the far wall and the low kitchen wall, facing the television and fire respectively. There are pictures on the walls and a rocking chair between the couches.

And there, on the far couch with reddened eyes and a bloody bandage on his shoulder...

Adrenaline dumps from my system. I nearly fall over, but with a growl, I stick my gun in my waistband, march across the living room, and stop short in front of Damen.

Carmen moves with me, her gaze locked on my movements. I barely notice her in my peripheral as I take in the boy I trained.

"Miss Belle, I..." His voice is strained as he slowly stands. He's shorter than me by several inches. Salty tear tracks stain his dark cheeks. Bruises and swelling mar his lips and eye.

My breath catches, eyes burning. I throw my arms around him, careful of his shoulder, and pull him to me. Biting down on my lip, I draw blood and don't let the tears fall.

Still, I can't help the hitch in my voice as I murmur in his ear, "Don't you ever do something like that again. You hear me?"

He nods against my shoulder. Hands wrap around my waist, and he squeezes. His grip is weak, shaky.

A moment passes and then Missa moves forward. "I need a hug too, Damen."

I release him and step back as she takes my place. I turn to Carmen. Maria and Rosie have emerged from the rooms down the hall and now stand at the edge of the living room. Rosie wears the same neutral expression I remember from three years ago. She's always seemed the steadiest of their little family.

Maria gives me a look that suggests I've grown horns or cursed in church. Possibly both.

My gaze slips past her to meet Damen's twin. "Anything out of the ordinary this morning?"

Her tone is dry. "Besides you? No."

I nod. "I still want to get you all to the safe-house."

Carmen's lips twitch into a crooked grin. "I figured. We're packed."

"We can probably take all of you in our rental." I glance toward the front door. My neck itches; that feeling of being watched creeps up my spine.

"I'll take Mama and Rosie in my car," Carmen says. She glances at her brother. "I'm sure you have some things to talk about. We can follow you."

I twist my lips to the side. Unease bubbles in my gut. "We should stay together."

"I'll be right behind you." Carmen catches my eye. There's something in her expression that halts me from protesting further. Her eyes dart to her mother, then back to me.

Ahh, she also has some things to talk about. I heave a sigh but agree.

"Damen." Missa's voice is soft, her hands gentle as she holds his arm. "Are you all right coming with us?"

He glances at me, and I catch that look I get from the Guides sometimes. The nervous expression like they're about to be in trouble. Honestly, he should be in trouble, but I can't get past the bloody bandage on his shoulder and the bruises covering his face. I'm sure there's more. Anytime you can see an injury like that, there's always more hidden from sight.

I force a smile to my lips, but it comes across stiff.

"Let's get going then." Carmen lifts two bags from behind the couch and marches out the front door.

The next hour consists of driving to the safe-house, unloading the bags, (as well as chickens, rabbits, and one very pregnant cat), and explaining the situation to the Joneses. Diego Jones, a massive black ex-cop from Chicago with a knack for woodworking, is getting on in years. When his wife mentioned retiring down south he called me up to see if there were any locations in which I could use an asset. That happened to be right around the time everything went down with Damen and Buccero. Diego and his wife, Loretta, moved to Peru and settled down outside of Arequipa.

They welcome us with open arms. Their home is massive. A two-story log cabin built by Diego over the course of a year. He hired enough local help to earn him a position of status in the community and kept on the laborers during a lumber shortage that would have cost them a lot of income. Instead, he had them do detail work for six weeks.

I grip the rail hard as I climb the steps to the wrap-around porch. The wood is soft, a fine grain stained to keep the rain from damaging it. Patterns of clouds, snowfall, pine trees—a full Hallmark Christmas card—is carved into the dang thing. The walls are the same, the heavy logs covered in intricate beauty.

Loretta brings us all in, sweeping arms ushering the group like we're her little ducklings. Rosie and Maria follow her up a massive staircase to the second floor. Carmen pops up to drop off her bag, then returns to the ground floor and settles onto a patterned couch next to Damen.

He has barely spoken. The drive here was quiet. I had plenty to say, but each time I glanced in the rear-view mirror and saw his face I couldn't get the words out. Instead, Missa filled him in on what's going on at the Manor. The cops, the bug, the frustration we all feel at being under the microscope.

She said some other stuff. Told Damen he should talk to Doc about how he's feeling. I shifted out at that point, let my mind wander through a list of plans for the next few days. Let my hands and feet control the car while I focused on not listening to all the very good reasons Missa has for someone to talk to a psychiatrist.

"What's next, Miss Belle?" Diego's deep voice, baritone and beautiful, breaks me from my distracted staring out their kitchen window.

It's a sliding door, leading to the far side of the wrap-around porch. Their house is perched on the edge of a cliff, looking out onto a stunning view. Mountains stretch ahead of us, snow-capped and massive. Arequipa itself sits in the plains a bit of a drive from here, which only adds to this position as a safe-house. Sweeping vegetation paints everything green. There has been rain recently.

"I'm not sure just yet," I say.

Missa, having just stepped into the kitchen with Loretta right behind her, raises an eyebrow at me.

I shrug at her and turn to Diego. "There's more to do here. I thought things were finished three years ago, but clearly that's not the case. I can't leave a job half-done." I flash half a grin. "You know that."

"I do," Diego agrees. "How long do you plan on staying then?"

I sigh. "A few days. Maybe longer. If you give me a few minutes with Damen I can give you a more precise answer."

"Yes, Diego." Loretta steps up, putting a hand on her husband's arm. "Let them settle in before you go trying to kick them out."

Diego opens his mouth, a slightly horrified expression on his face as he begins to object.

"No, no, no." Loretta's grin widens, and she winks at me. "You've been rude enough. Let's get some food going for our guests and then you can pester them after lunch."

I leave the kitchen, chuckling as Diego protests his wife's take on the whole situation.

Carmen and Damen go silent as I step into the living room. Two massive couches and a pair of comfy armchairs form a crescent around a brick fireplace and mantle. Bookshelves line either side, full of hardbacks, knickknacks, and trinkets.

It's the sort of room one could spend hours in without knowing time has passed at all. Handmade wooden coffee tables rest between each of the couches. A large one normally sits in the center. It has been pulled to the couch Damen and Carmen sit at. Papers coat the top.

I walk around the furniture, aware of the twins' eyes on me. Bending at the waist, I take in the work before them.

Blueprints. A badly drawn map. A list of names, numbered guards, weapons, ammunition, mileage, and possible hide-outs. The pages are coated in question marks. Scribbles.

It looks like a child's art project.

Damen swallows and opens his mouth, watching me. I hold up a hand.

Behind him, Missa leans over the couch, looking between the twins' heads to study the paperwork as well.

"Interesting," she murmurs.

"Interesting, indeed." I pull one of the armchairs over, settle in, and lean forward. I reach out and take one of the papers. It's a rough hand-drawn map of a compound—a villa—little markings for guards, lights, and gates.

I glance up and meet Damen's gaze. "It looks like you're not done here."

His fingers move, slide along the chain at his neck like they always do when he's anxious. He tugs the crucifix forward and rubs it between his thumb and finger. "Not until he's dead, Miss Belle."

I watch him for a long moment, reading the look in his eye. My mind jumps to calculations, contemplating what an endeavor like this will entail. But I push those away for the moment. Instead, I focus on this boy before me. A man really, at this point. He was a boy when I met him. When I realized the rumors surrounding Buccero were true. When I watched old press conferences. Saw the way Damen moved when Buccero touched his arm. Saw the fury hiding in his eyes. The same fury I see now—no longer hidden.

I nod.

Damen leans back, eyes wide. "You're not going to try to stop us?"

I glance up at Missa. She exhales, long and slow before coming around to sit on the other side of Carmen.

"No." I look back to Damen. "But we should talk before you go too far into this plan."

"About what?" Carmen cuts in.

My gaze darts to her for a second. "About what it means to take someone's life. It's not something Damen has had to do before now, and it's not..."

"It's not as easy as it seems," Missa fills in.

I nod again.

"I'm re—"

I put up a hand to silence Damen. He falls quiet immediately, and Carmen raises her eyebrows.

"There's a difference, Damen, between killing someone for justice and killing someone for revenge. You need to know that difference before you pull the trigger. You need to know you can handle it before the deed is done. Because once you do it, there's no going back."

Damen stares down at the table before him. He releases the cross and his hands, knuckles bruised in a way that sparks pride in my chest, fidget before him.

"How about for both?" Carmen asks. "This." She gestures to the tabletop, to the plans they made.

Plans which, by the look of them, would get these two killed in a matter of minutes. I don't say that though. I let her finish.

"This is both." Her jaw goes tight. The same sharp edge her brother has. "Buccero needs to die. Not only for my brother's revenge, but because a man like that cannot be allowed to continue his destruction of our country."

Warmth seeps from my chest through my limbs. I rub my fingers against my palms, then clap my hands together and lean forward, a smile creeping across my face. "Both..." I glance at Missa. She nods. My mind yanks those calculations, plans, ideas, back to the forefront. I look at Damen. "Both is ideal. Let's get to work."

Planning happens at the Jones's. Maria and Rosie stay out of the way for the most part. Maria still looks at me as though I'm conspiring with the devil rather than against him. Our relationship was rocky enough when all I did was take her little boy to a distant country to be an "art buyer." I don't think Damen ever told her the truth of what he'd be doing. I don't blame him, and it's better for our business if as few people know the details as possible.

I could probably ease the tension. Probably talk things out, find out why she's so wary of me. Find out why she pulls Rosie from the room when she finds the two of us talking. But my ribs still sting. My throat catches at the thunks of Diego chopping wood out back. My blood races, boils, at the slightest conflict.

I avoid her.

Carmen has a surprisingly large store of knowledge about Buccero and his company. She drops Damen's jaw when she pulls up a document on her laptop—a complete list of his stock holdings, company covers, the name of every man on his board of directors, and the names of each person/company he has been selling off land to—most of them from the States.

"How is he getting around the government regulations?" Damen asks.

Carmen rolls her eyes at the same time I'm tempted to do the same. Missa is gentler. She leans her hands against the pale wood of the kitchen table, studying the documents.

"Money."

I nod, clenching my jaw to avoid the "duh" that wants to come out. Missa points, her finger running down a spreadsheet of ledgers with Buccero's finances. How did Carmen get them? Well, she's been a bit cagey regarding all the information she has access to. It's bringing out both admiration and fury in me.

"There are protests going on up north," Carmen says. She moves aside a ledger and pulls a map of Peru forward. She points to a ridge of mountains lining the Amazon. "This is where the majority of the native populations live. The villages are remote, hard to get to, and not great for tourism. Buccero tosses some cash to the Bureau of Native Land Management and he can sweep through, pretending he owns the land. None of it is real. A smoke screen he's using to sell everything off to American investors. But by the time he has to go about getting the actual permits to buy the land—"

"There's no one there to object to the purchase," I interrupt. I run a hand across my chin. "How?"

Carmen grits her teeth. I stare at her across the table, my gaze unwavering.

"How do you know all this, Carmen? This is more than *we've* been able to access." I gesture to Missa and myself. "What's your source?"

Carmen glares. I glare back. Damen clears his throat. We both ignore him, the staring contest consuming our attention—or at least mine.

Carmen breaks away. She moves from the table, and I'm tempted to follow, but Missa puts up a hand. I grimace, nod, and walk the opposite direction. The outdoors is calling me. I slide the glass door open, step onto the porch, and stride to the railing. The wind picks up my hair.

Thoughts roll through my head. The list of places Buccero owns is long. Five properties scattered across Peru. The optimal place to attack is his home, the villa in Arequipa. It's not an option anymore. A simple drive-by showed enough soldiers to catch even Missa. Not because they'd see her, but because she'd be liable to bump into one, they're so jam-packed into the space.

His office front in the north is the next best, but it's so remote... He's hardly there—according to Carmen—and when he is, there are dozens of innocents protesting the building. Too many bodies. Too much potential for collateral damage.

How?

That's the question I keep coming back to.

How do we do this in a way that won't come back to bite any of us in the ass? Or, you know, toss us into a prison cell for the rest of our lives?

I could call in the cavalry. Get Janette, Sarah—no, she started an assignment yesterday. Josie? But she's busy prepping for this summer. Alex and Anita would be ideal, especially since Anita speaks fluent Spanish, and they could both pass for Peruvians if one wasn't looking hard enough.

Missa and I discussed it yesterday.

The wind picks up. A chill runs down my bare arms, the little hairs standing on end. I straighten. Leaning on the rail too long hurts my ribs.

Why is this so hard? Why is it too much? There's been more—there's usually more—going on than right now. I suppose part of it might be the police. I'm not particularly worried about all of us getting hauled into jail in New York, but the constant presence has gone beyond annoying.

I also feel incredibly stupid for allowing that damn cop into the Manor. My lack of awareness weighs on me. I can't afford it. Not in this line of work.

"Hey."

I don't turn. Missa joins me at the rail, leaning against it with the wind billowing against her long braid.

"What was that about?" she murmurs, not looking at me.

I shrug.

"You're worried we won't be able to pull this off."

A muscle in my jaw twitches as I clench my teeth. This woman knows me too well.

"We definitely need help. The four of us can't do this ourselves. It's going to take more manpower than we have access to."

My gaze slides to her. To her blue eyes staring out at the landscape. Her tone is casual, but I hear part of what she's saying. She doesn't want me going in. She wants me in the van, on look-out, part of the exterior team.

A moment passes, me watching her, her watching the trees blow. Then she turns.

"Carmen has contacts."

I nod.

"What if we asked them for help?"

I click my teeth, then bite my lower lip. I rub my forehead, that little divot where a bullet grazed me a few weeks ago...

"Yeah. Let's do that."

Chapter Sixteen

Damen

Sister's Secrets

I follow Carmen after Miss Belle walks away from the table. My twin is in her room on the second floor of the Jones's house. I push the door open, stride across the space, and sink onto her bed.

Pain radiates from my shoulder. The meds I took this morning are starting to wear off. I roll my head, stretching my neck with a groan.

"Are you okay?" Carmen asks from her perch by the window. She's sitting on the wide sill, staring outside and not looking at me.

"I'll live. This time."

She shakes her head, turning to catch my eye. "That's not funny."

A painful smile pulls at my split lip. "It's not *not* funny."

Carmen heaves a disgruntled—maybe disgusted—sigh. "Your boss is an asshole."

This time a chuckle bursts out, and I wince. "Don't make me laugh."

"Why is she so persistent?" Carmen grunts. She crosses from the window and sinks onto the bed next to me. "I have information we need. Why pester me about where I got it?"

I hesitate. It's been three years since I met Miss Belle. In that time, I've learned so much from her, but I've yet to figure out how she ticks. Still, given everything we've talked about for this mission, and her state after getting back from Thailand, I have an idea as to why she isn't letting this go.

"We need help."

Carmen raises an eyebrow at me. I nod.

"This was supposed to be quick. In and out, and he'd be dead. Now... it's going to be a lot harder. I'm injured. Miss Belle is recovering from injuries. Besides that, he'll be expecting us. We don't have the numbers we need to make this happen without a lot of noise. I think..." I rub my thumb against my palm with a grimace. "I think she's going to ask you if you know anyone who can help."

Carmen closes her eyes, drawing a hand through her coarse black hair.

"What's going on with you, Carmen?" I ask. "How *do* you have all this information?"

She rises from the bed, rubbing her hand across her forehead with a sigh. "We were supposed to be laying low. I know..." She utters a growl, strides to the door, and closes it. "Mama made me promise. Me and Rosie, that we wouldn't cause any trouble. We wouldn't stir things up and have to move again." She stares at me for a moment, her eyes—the same as mine—bore into me. "You can't tell her."

I nod.

Then Carmen explains. She tells me about the native villages along the Amazon border. She tells me how she's been driving there every week to spend a few days reading to the women in those villages. She's been teaching them Spanish.

Helping them learn to write, learn to read, learn to run their own businesses and be independent.

"You remember what Papa used to say about our Abuela, that the only thing slowing her down was where she was born. I didn't—" Her fist clenches at her side. "Mama kept getting on me about going back to school. But this is such a better use of my time. I'm making a difference, Damen."

I bite the inside of my lip. "What about the information?"

She heaves a sigh. "The villages I've been helping... that's where Buccero is trying to steal the land. He set up offices there. He has a voice on the village councils. He's already driven one of the villages from their land."

I wince. "That's horrible."

"Yeah. Yeah it is. So we've been protesting."

I close my eyes with a pained grimace. "Protesting?" I cross to the window, rubbing my forehead. "That's not exactly keeping under the radar, Carmen."

"As opposed to you?" she snaps.

A tense silence fills the room for a moment.

"So the protests?" I prompt. "I'm assuming there are people working with you to set things up and keep it going?"

Carmen nods. "You had a plan to kill Buccero. We are going for something different. We are trying to get enough evidence to permanently destroy his company."

I exhale, watching the wind blow through the trees outside. "How many?"

"There's one woman I'll call. If she can come, she'll bring people. However many we can spare from the protest line."

I'm right. Later that night, Miss Belle asks Carmen if she has any contacts who might be able to help with the infiltration. My sister gets on the phone and about ten minutes later, returns to the room with good news. Our help arrives by morning.

Auntie—that's what Carmen is calling her, I have no idea what her real name is—is a formidable woman. She's short with weathered dark skin, wrinkled around her eyes and mouth. She wears long sleeves and hefty military-style pants. I spot a hilt coming up the side of one of her boots. Her hair is tied off in a long black braid. When the front door opens to let her in, her gaze scans the interior of the home—spending a fraction longer on the exits—before she looks to Miss Belle.

Carmen moves to her, sharing a quick hug before she makes introductions. Through the still open door, a heavy truck holds a number of curious faces peeking toward the house.

"Miss Belle?" Auntie steps up, hand out.

Miss Belle takes it with a nod. "Pleasure. Your reputation precedes you, *Auntie.*"

"As does yours," Auntie says with a smirk.

Miss Belle chuckles. "Don't believe everything you've heard."

"Nor you."

An eyebrow raises as Miss Belle cocks her head. "Are you saying you *didn't* take out a dozen mercs in Iraq just before they were able to blow that satellite station?"

During the subsequent pause, I give Carmen a meaningful look. She shrugs one shoulder, casting an infuriating *you'll see* look my way.

"You have done your research," Auntie says.

Miss Belle's smile deepens. "You're one of the most dangerous women on the planet. I'd be remiss not to take some lessons. Even if they are in the form of redacted mission statements."

Auntie raises her eyebrows at Carmen. "I like this one; I'm glad you introduced us."

Carmen gives a tight smile.

In no time, we have to leave. There are a couple reasons for our departure. The first, we shouldn't stay in Arequipa. The Jones's are kind enough to let us hide out in their home as long as we need, but unnecessarily putting them in danger because I failed doesn't sit well with me. When Miss Belle suggested renting a house on the coast near Lima, I was all for it.

The second reason? Buccero's offices are in Lima. They're where we are going to hit him. Hard. Fast. No mercy.

Chapter Seventeen

Miss Belle

Seeing Red

"I'm a little honored," I murmur to Missa as we pull onto the highway.

"Why?" she asks, absentmindedly staring out the passenger window.

We are Lima-bound. The twins are in Carmen's car with Maria and Rosie. Auntie took her men—six in total—in their truck. That left Missa and me in our rental. Diego tried to join, but I reminded him that we need a back-up in case things go way too wrong.

It's a long damn drive to Peru's capital city, but there are enough people that we can drive through the night and arrive in the morning.

I wanted to leave Maria and Rosie with the Jones's as well, but Damen's face when I suggested it broke my heart. So they're coming with us. The house Missa found is a fair drive from Lima. A good thirty minutes outside of the city, along the coastal cliffs. They should be safe there.

All the same, with the looks Maria has been giving me since we arrived, I was hoping to not be in the same house as her for a little while.

"Auntie knows about me," I say. "She knows about us, the organization." I do a little dance, fingers tapping across the steering wheel. "Miss Belle's Travel Guides."

"She thinks we're whores." The words are harsh, but her tone is light. She grins at me. Teasing.

"She doesn't know *what* to think now." I laugh.

It was a shock, the knock at the door, Diego opening it to reveal one of the most deadly women on the planet. She can handle every type of gun made. Her skills with a blade are legendary. Her hand to hand would knock my ass out in about twenty seconds.

Auntie was a soldier in the Peruvian army. She spent years working up the ranks, taking out the Shining Path, a communist group from the 80s and 90s that had a penchant for killing civilians. When they were finally defeated, and no longer attacking innocent villages, she stayed in the line of work.

The U.S. has a lot of contractors in the Middle East, and Auntie was one of them. Her nickname with the Peruvian army, Tia, was latched onto by American GIs. They 'merica'd it up, and she's gone by Auntie ever since.

A couple of the trainers we work with during a girl's first year got their hand-to-hand lessons from her. The kind of intensive, invaluable training it appears Carmen has been getting for the past year or so.

I'm a little jealous.

"So," Missa says, "get to the house, figure out everyone's position, then take down a multimillion-dollar corporation and kill the CEO?"

I give a thoughtful nod. "Grocery shopping first when we get to the house. But besides that, yeah, sounds like a plan."

The house is large. I give Missa a side-eye once the car comes to a stop on the dusty gravel out front. A European style build, there is a massive front door lined by columns, high windows, and probably enough bedrooms to give everyone their own—including Auntie's men.

"How much was this place?" I open the door and am greeted by the sound of the ocean waves crashing against the cliffs. Succulents and long native grasses cover the grounds. It's like something out of a painting.

"I'm not telling." Missa shuts her door and comes around the front of the car, her arms crossed against the breeze. "We have the funds for it, and Damen deserves a nice place to spend some time with his family."

"And you don't like planning heists in anything but the height of comfort." My tone is dry, but there's a smile on my lips.

She shrugs. "I did my time in crappy motels. We can afford style, I'm getting style."

My laugh is torn away by a heavy wind.

The others arrive within twenty minutes. I, uh... I was driving, which had a bit of an impact on how quickly we got here. By the time Damen pushes through the door, I'm at the massive wooden dining table, spreading out every scrap of paper we have while Missa sets up the monitors. Three screens: 3D blueprints of Buccero's office building, online applications for a few of our new friends to fill out, and

Buccero's public schedule. The man thinks he's a politician. His daily activities are mostly accounted for in the press release his assistant sends out every morning. An idiotic waste of time but helpful for us.

Auntie plants her hands at her waist and surveys what we are working with. "All right, Miss Belle." She glances at me. "What is the plan?"

I step forward, but a twinge in my gut reminds me that this isn't my project. This isn't my revenge, my people, my country. So, I gesture to Damen.

He rubs his palms together and inhales. "The plan is to kill Vincente Buccero. The man is corrupt. Evil. He needs to die."

Beside him, Carmen nods fervently. Auntie raises an eyebrow at her.

"Truly, Auntie," she says. "Our protests aren't enough. The man cannot be allowed to continue as he has."

Auntie raises a finger. The tip of it is gnarled, scarred over where it was cut off at the nail. She points it at Carmen, expectation in the lines on her face. "What of the company?"

Carmen hesitates. She glances at her brother.

I fold my arms, waiting. I'd love to jump in here, but Missa and I agreed to let Damen figure out this lesson on his own. Buccero isn't a general on a battlefield. He's not a warlord commanding civilians. Cutting the head off the snake won't do much in this particular case.

"What of it?" Damen asks. "Buccero will be gone."

"Young man," Auntie's voice is cold, "Vincente Buccero was in prison for the last three years. That's as gone as it is possible to get without a headstone. It did nothing to stop his company from continuing their exploitation of the native peoples of Peru. His influence does not stop simply because he is gone. His company is a rot, a disease. We need more than one bullet to end the injustice he spreads."

"Does that mean…" Carmen says slowly.

"We need to kill everyone in the company?" Damen finishes for her, horror on his face.

"*No,*" Auntie and I both interject loudly. We share an alarmed look.

"What is wrong with you, Damen?" I grumble. "No. It sounds like this will be a two-pronged mission. One prong"—I point to Damen—"to kill the man." I raise my eyebrows as my gaze turns to Carmen. "The other, to find what we need to take down his company."

The week flies by.

Within a few days, there are men positioned on three different levels of Buccero's office building. One in the security department, one as an IT specialist, and one as a janitor. There was a fair amount of fighting over who went for which job, but in the end, Carmen sarcastically reminded them that these were temporary gigs. They'd last a couple weeks—at most.

Missa nearly fell over laughing when one grumbled that they didn't want their resume ruined, and Auntie cuffed his ear saying, "You're using a false identity, Carlos. This isn't going on your resume!"

Rosie has interjected herself into the plans, much to my and Maria's discomfort. She offers to run surveillance, something we have trouble saying no to as it gets closer and closer to game-day with a limited number of bodies to eyeball Buc-cero's building.

I also itch to leave the house. Beyond morning walks along the coast, bundled all to heck to stay warm in the wind, I'm not leaving the property much. Missa's doing. She has been in charge of the scheduling and is clearly keeping me home—insisting there is no need for me to go into Lima.

The edge of the city is only thirty minutes away. She's gone five times between grocery trips, running surveillance, and shopping. I do look fantastic in my new alpaca sweater. It's very warm.

"So, I'm saying," Rosie cocks her head at me the same way Damen does when he wants something, "I don't see why we can't do surveillance tomorrow and pick up groceries on the way home. People keep forgetting my almond milk. Besides," she crosses her arms, "I know you want to get out of this house as much as I do. No way Carmen lets me go alone."

"She's right," I say, my mind elsewhere as I pore over blueprints. There's the matter of this elevator shaft...

"Carlos and Louis can't do their shift tomorrow. Carlos is starting at the IT department and Louis's wife went into labor this morning. He's catching the next plane back to Pucallpa."

"Hmm." I nod, biting my lip without really listening.

"Well, if you won't come with me, I'll ask Missa."

"Wait." I pull myself from the screen and wheel the chair around to face her. "I'll take you." I roll my pen across my knuckles and then point the tip at her. "But you have to tell Missa."

"I'll tell Missa if you tell Carmen."

The grin spreads across my face. "You're cleverer than your brother, ya know that?"

She nods. "Don't tell him though."

I laugh. "I wasn't planning on it."

The next morning finds the two of us leaving at dawn. I feel like a teenager allowed to go to a friend's party or something. Mom—Missa—watches from the front door, her arms crossed as I pull down the driveway.

The drive into the city is quiet. Early morning traffic is nothing like it will be later. I get honked at a few times. I'm driving like I'm from the States. Sue me, I like using street lines.

Still, we get to Miraflores district without incident. I pull into a parking garage, park near the exit, and head to the nearest coffee shop. The night shift on watch (Auntie and Carmen) will be leaving in the next half hour or so. Gives us plenty of time to grab a snack and head over.

This type of surveillance doesn't need to be a constant presence, but it's important to get an idea of Buccero's habits. What things on his agenda he sticks to, and where he deviates. Who shows up to the building late, which workers bring food, who they send on coffee runs midway through the morning. As many details as possible will help the operation run smoothly.

The latte hits the spot, as does a blueberry muffin and a to-go box of potato wedges. The office building—a massive bulky thing in the center of the business district—is across the street from a lovely little park. Fountain, benches, some cute grassy areas, and a plethora of business folks grabbing a quick bite outdoors before they have to get to work.

We settle onto a bench with a good view of the building. I lean against the slatted wood and stretch my neck. The ribs are better. I still feel the bruising when I try anything high impact. An attempted jog the other day ended after about a mile. Which is further than I've been able to go in weeks, but still annoying.

"So..." Rosie begins after a few minutes of quietly sipping on coffee. "Why were you benched?"

She can't see the glare under my bug-eyed sunglasses, but it's there. "I wasn't benched."

"Come on."

I jerk back a little at her tone. It's so familiar. So similar to her brother with that cajoling lilt to her English.

"You've been at the house as much as I have. Everyone else is coming in and out all the time. Even Mama went to the town up north for groceries with Carmen a few days ago. You and I are the only ones who haven't been allowed to leave."

There's a low growl in my voice as I respond, "I was allowed to leave. I wasn't needed for surveillance."

"There's more to it," Rosie insists, ignoring my tone. "What's the deal?"

With a clenched jaw, I set my coffee on the ground and rub my fingers together to warm them up. "I got injured on my last trip. Bruised ribs. Missa has been mother-henning me since I got back."

A smile splits the girl's face. "I knew there was something."

"Yes," I say dryly, "you're very clever."

"What does that mean for the actual..." she looks around furtively and leans in, whispering, "heist?"

My irritation is alleviated by amusement. "I'll be on comms. Your siblings are going to need someone in the van giving them instructions and keeping an eye on the building, traffic footage, police scanners. All that sort of thing."

Rosie nods. "And Missa will be with you for that?"

"I think so," I say. "The smaller the better for the inside team. Auntie has her assignment once things get started. Ensuring a clean exit is key, better to have two groups on it."

"And me?"

I stifle the chortle that bursts from my lips. Rosie glares.

"You'll be at the house," I say, my tone firm. "Making sure your Mama stays away from the news stations and keeping yourself out of danger."

I expect an outburst of some kind. Whining like her brother would. Fighting me like Carmen would. Instead, Rosie is quiet for a long moment.

When she speaks, her voice is so low I have to lean in to hear her. "I don't want to see Damen like that again."

My stomach clenches. I bite the inside of my lower lip, knowing exactly how she feels and knowing my words here will do very little to ease her worry. Still...

"Your brother is a very capable individual." I put a hand on her arm. "He made a mistake. Anger does that—causes mistakes. This time, he has a whole crew behind him. Seasoned people who know what they're doing, help with the planning, and emergency exits in case something goes bad." I raise my hand from her arm and point at her. "Always, I repeat, *always* have an exit strategy." I shake my head. "Damen should have known better."

She swallows. "I was worried... when he told us what happened, I was worried maybe he didn't want to escape."

A dull ache permeates my chest. Around us, flurries of movement distract my attention. A few pigeons peck at crumbs. Two men walk by, gesticulating wildly as they discuss some dumb thing. A child sprints across a grassy patch with no worry of falling.

"I don't think that's what he wanted," I say. "He could have died on that bridge. Could have stayed in the river and let it end that way."

"He was so ashamed when he talked to Mama."

Confusion ripples through the burning concern within. "When?"

"Right before you arrived." Rosie picks at the remains of her muffin. "I already knew most of it but..." she shakes her head, staring off into the distance. "Mama never knew what he did to Damen."

I don't need to ask who *he* is.

"She never knew how Damen feels about other men."

My jaw tightens. I know how much Maria loves her children, but she's a very Catholic woman. "How did she handle that part?"

Rosie sighs. "Fine, I guess. She was more upset he hadn't told her before now. Part of her blames you."

"For him being bi?"

"For all of it." She shakes her head. "It doesn't make sense."

A bitter smile crosses my lips. "It's easier to blame me than it is to recognize how little she knew about her own son. I don't mind." I lean down for my coffee, clenching the cup a little too tight and spilling some on my cream-colored jeans.

A chunk of time passes. I focus on breathing. Rosie writes notes about the ins and outs of the office building. At noon, a stack of pizzas is delivered. I tell her to make a note of which shop they ordered from.

"So," I say after returning from a quick pee break at a nearby shop. "Nursing school?"

Rosie flushes and dips her head in a nod. "It's expensive, but Mama has put all the money Damen sends in an account for him. She thinks he'll come back and buy a house some-day."

I chuckle. "Sounds like something my mom would do."

Rosie blinks a few times and gapes at me.

"What?"

"It's... sorry. I just never thought of you as having parents."

I squint at her, my tone incredulous. "You know I'm not a robot, right?"

She laughs. "Yeah, yeah sorry. It's odd to think of you as a kid."

I tilt my head in agreement. "That's fair. Anyway, you were talking about nursing school and money?"

"Right." She straightens a little. I can see the Catholic in the rigidity of her spine, the way the hard wooden bench hasn't stunted her posture in the slightest. "Well, Carmen had the idea to ask Mama to use some of it to pay for nursing classes." She smiles.

It almost hurts, seeing the hope in her eyes, the excitement on her face. A future of endless possibilities. A future to fight for.

A pit grows in my gut. Dark and rotting.

"Aren't you seventeen?" I blurt out.

Rosie bobs her head. "I graduated last year. If I plan things right, I can start nursing school in a year or two. It depends on which classes are available this fall. I've got almost all of the required units."

"Impressive." I meant it to be kind, but it comes out in a mumble.

Rosie takes my tone in stride with a shrug. "I've worked hard."

I don't respond, not trusting what might come out of my mouth. These spiteful thoughts don't need to be voiced to an innocent girl who really has worked hard. I know because I've kept track.

I also have an account set up for her nursing school. She doesn't need to know about that though. Carmen will deal with the finances when the time comes.

The rest of our shift passes in relative quiet. We walk around a bit, taking turns going to the bathroom, getting food, and watching the exits.

Eventually, it's time to leave. The sun has dipped to the edge of the horizon. Two of Auntie's men move into the square as we make our way toward the parking garage. Rosie gives them a wave before I take gentle hold of her wrist and lower her hand. She offers up a sheepish, apologetic grin.

"Groceries?" I say. We passed a market on our way to the square this morning; should be easy enough to stop by and get her nut milk on the way back to the car.

"Yes." Rosie perks up and quickens her pace. "Mama wanted me to pick up a few things too."

Thirty minutes later, I'm barely containing my heavy sighs as Rosie finishes checking out. So much for a quick stop. The sky is lit with color now—bright reds, purples, and pinks as the sun hits a layer of clouds on the horizon.

Rosie's arms are full. Two bags dangling from each wrist and a loaf of bread cradled in her arms like a baby.

I've got two bags as well. A frustrating thing, really, because my hands are itching to be free. Itching to be ready in case something goes wrong. My nerves haven't settled. I was hoping a trip to the city would help. Maybe I just needed to get out of the house. Maybe I needed a change of scenery. A change of pace.

My gaze flicks from side to side, watching the dark shadows on the street. There are a lot of shadows. Streetlights beam down, but still. Anxiety roils in my gut.

Rosie doesn't seem to notice. Her smile is pronounced as she talks about spending tomorrow baking *alfajores* cookies in between her study sessions. I vaguely realize this is why she spent so long shopping. Eggs, butter, powdered sugar... now I get why I'm bogged down with a five lb bag of flour.

The foot traffic has eased. Most people have found their way to their cars, their evening jobs, and plans. There is the occasional dart of someone going from a vehicle to a shop or restaurant, but the streets are clear for the most part.

Which is why the looming shadow of a man standing under a streetlight across the way catches my attention. I watch him, eyeing the way his gaze doesn't look at me once. He's focused on Rosie.

"Let's pick up the pace," I murmur.

Rosie's eyes widen. She was mid-explanation about the best way to get the *manjor blanco* (a thick caramelly sauce) to sit between the cookies to make a nice little sandwich. I should introduce her to Sarah; they could cook together.

She nods. "This'll be quicker."

I follow her gesture to a dark alley between two somewhat shorter buildings. We're still in the skyscraper section of the city, but these are restaurants, only a couple stories tall.

"Hmm," I grumble.

It will be faster. This alley cuts the block in half, chopping down our route to the parking garage by a full block.

Footsteps sound behind us. I glance back. The man has crossed the street. Looking ahead, the road is clear. There is light but no foot traffic to get lost in.

"All right. Let's go."

Rosie skips ahead, striding down the alley, perfectly at ease. Heat spreads behind my ears and at the back of my neck.

"Hey."

There it is. My jaw clenches. Rosie starts to turn.

"Nope," I say. "Keep walking."

"Hey, *linda*," the man says. His feet pound the pavement as he catches up to us. He continues in Spanish, ignoring me and gazing at every inch of Rosie's body.

A prickle of burning crawls up my spine.

"Where are you going in such a hurry?"

I move to Rosie's side, keeping her against the wall as we walk even faster now, ignoring him. Her eyes are wide as her gaze meets mine. I give a little nod.

"Hey." He reaches out. Grasps between us for her elbow.

I jerk to the side, my arm slamming into his hand. He curses, and I wheel around. "There's nothing for you here," I snap in Spanish. "Leave us alone."

His scowl is visible in the light pouring in from the street. We've made it most of the way through the alley now. Rosie hesitates, seemingly unsure if she should keep going without me. I hook my arm around hers and march us toward the street.

It happens quick, his reaching out, taking hold of her free arm, and pulling. The bread hits the ground. One of the grocery bags rips and blueberries scatter across the pavement.

Rosie lets out a sound. Surprise and pain.

I drop my bags. I drop her arm. I drop the thin veil that's been keeping everything in check. Keeping *me* in check.

"Let her go." It comes out as a growl. What this man wants with Rosie… what Buccero did to Damen… what so many men have done to so many people I care about.

His hand loosens. Rosie rips from his grasp.

He says something vile as he spits at her feet.

Heat slams through me. Tinges of red fill the edges of my vision. My hands clench, knuckles itching to sting.

I swing.

My fist connects with his face, and he lurches to the side. He comes back with a punch to my gut, but I'm ready for it. I grab his arm and twist. My body weight goes into the move. He hits the ground.

I leap for him, punching again. My right fist knocks his face to one side. My left lands another blow returning him to center.

My knees have him pinned, holding his arms against the ground as I swing. Over and over. Sound is gone. Thought is gone. My knuckles hurt. Blood hits my face, adding to the red that has consumed my sight.

They can't keep doing this. They can't keep assuming they're owed.

Images assault me. Damen, tears running down his face in the back of the coffee shop where I offered him freedom from Buccero. Lacey, the bruises marring her skin when Missa and I arrived at the home she'd been in for years, protecting her sister. The girl from that village in Laos.

Blood. These men deserve nothing but blood.

Something hits my perception. A sound of fear.

I blink, startled backward in horror at the thought that someone has gotten to Rosie while I've been...

I jerk up and off the man, a bloody pulp where his face should be. My gaze darts around the alley, searching for signs of danger.

Rosie is there, clenching her remaining grocery bags to her chest. Fear clouds her eyes but... but she's looking at me.

I step forward, "Are you—"

Her stumble backward is like a knife to my gut.

The red is gone. Replaced with a gray sort of filter as I take a moment to assess. My hands are coated with blood. My knuckles split, the pale flesh already bruising. I swallow. My mouth is so dry.

On the ground, moaning—so still alive—is the man who'd grabbed Rosie.

My breath is short. Shallow.

I swallow again. Without another word to Rosie, I bend and pick up the bags and the bread. The blueberries are done. Squished into the asphalt.

She stares at me as I straighten and meet her eye. "Let's go."

Chapter Eighteen

Damen

Operation Don't-Fuck-it-Up

I look good in black. I prefer gray or white suits. Something with a trim, crisp and clean cut; no tie, or at least a full Windsor. Black feels too much like a funeral. Still...

I half-turn, scanning my reflection in the full-length mirror. I look damn good.

My shoes have high quality grip. My gloves are thin, perfect for not leaving fingerprints but also not encumbering my movement. My vest is thick, not bullet-proof, but enough extra padding to slow a knife. My belt and pants pockets are adorned with numerous useful items.

I caress the holster carrying my gun.

Tonight he dies.

"You done admiring yourself?" Carmen's dry voice sounds from the doorway to my left.

I turn from the mirror, rolling my eyes. "You're jealous I make this look better than you do."

Her dark eyes widen, a flash of annoyance making me grin. She's wearing a nearly identical outfit. With our similar features, our shared eyes, lips, and nose... we could almost be the same person.

Our missions tonight are not the same.

Miss Belle's voice hollers from downstairs. "It's time!"

Carmen's look shifts to anticipation. Worry. We exchange a glance and hurry to the car.

Lima is dark. Certain parts of the city are lively at night, but the business district isn't one of them. There are no clubs here. The restaurants close a little after the end of the workday.

Missa pulls the van we are using—a rental—to the far side of the road. The interior of the vehicle has been quiet during the drive here. Miss Belle isn't talking about the bruises on her knuckles. It's infuriating for Missa. Rosie refuses to say anything about what happened during their watch the other day, but she came back to the house pale as a sheet.

I glance at the women responsible for running a multi-million dollar business and spy network. Miss Belle catches my gaze for a moment, a little smile flicking across her lips. She rubs her hands together and leans forward.

"Everyone clear on the plan?"

The van is large. Carmen and I sit on one side, each holding a little box with our coms inside. Miss Belle is on the other, one laptop resting on her knees, another on the bench beside her. She and Missa will be out here, waiting.

Carmen and I nod. Miss Belle licks her lips.

"All right then. Auntie?" She adjusts the headset covering one of her ears. "Are you in place?"

A second passes before she nods.

"Let's do this. Remember, limited communication. Get in. Get out. Don't wait for each other."

Carmen squeezes my hand on the bench between us. We both nod again.

I open the back doors to the van, and we step out. A little park sits between us and Buccero's office building. A couple is kissing under one of the streetlights. I inhale, the chill in the spring night air shocking my lungs.

I glance at my sister. She finishes latching her com around her ear. I do the same.

I take a final look at the van, meeting Miss Belle's determined look. We share a nod.

Then Carmen and I stride toward the building.

One Week Ago

"Key cards are the fastest way to get in," Rodriguez says. He stands with his arms crossed, staring down at our blueprint of the first floor. "The security cameras are going to be the biggest problem. I can get you inside, and I can program a USB to stop them recording, but anyone looking at the screens will see you."

Louis, a shorter man with more muscle definition, stands. "That might not be a problem. I've got the night shift for the rest of the month. I knock out my partner and keep an eye on things while you two go to work." He nods to me and Carmen.

"Won't he point the finger at you once he wakes up?" I ask with a frown.

Miss Belle shakes her head, meeting Louis's eye. "That won't be an issue. Louis will have a large dose for his partner." She holds up an empty syringe, cap on the needle. "And a much smaller dose for himself. We time it right, and it'll look like they both got attacked. He quits after everything due to trauma."

"They'll buy that?" Carmen raises an eyebrow.

Louis laughs. "It doesn't really matter if they buy it or not. It's not like I put my real address on my resume."

Present

We scan through the door with the blank key card Rodriguez prepared. I stick it in my back pocket as Carmen walks ahead of me.

The lobby is dark. The large space is less gaudy than Buccero's usual decor. Simple but comfortable furniture fills the area, hardwood floors in square patterns, and a little coffee cart against one of the walls all offer a welcoming environment. A good facade for a man trying to fix a terrible reputation.

Dim lights from the elevator down the hall to the right, and the glowing screens at the front desk, are the only things permeating the black interior. A man sits behind the desk.

I follow Carmen forward. She spares Louis a glance and a nod. Beside him, on the floor, is an unconscious body.

Louis flashes me a wink as we pass by, making our way to the elevators.

My palms sweat into my gloves as the little arrow flashes down.

Carmen swallows. "You ready for this?" she murmurs.

I breathe out through pursed lips. I'm about to answer honestly, but I remember we are on coms with the whole team. Instead, I nod.

The elevator dings. We step on. We go up, my stomach churning, though not because of the movement.

We come to a stop at the 42nd floor, Buccero's office.

"You're good here?" I put a hand on her arm.

My sister nods. "I know what we need. I'll get it. Go finish the job."

She turns without another word, disappearing into the open seating area. Buccero's private office is in one of the corners. It takes up nearly a third of this floor.

I reach out and hit the button for 43. Buccero's home away from home.

One Week Ago

"During the day," Auntie agrees.

Across the table from them, Missa shakes her head. "That won't work. These two will stick out like sore thumbs. Shutting down the cameras won't matter if there are people all over the place."

"Buccero won't be there at night," Miss Belle reminds her. "He has his own condo in the city. Unless we can fake an emergency to draw him in..." She rubs her fingers across her forehead. "Or if something happened to the condo..."

Missa's eyes narrow, a smile curling up the side of her face. She turns to Marco, the one of Auntie's men who drew the janitor straw. "That top floor you were talking about... you say it's fully furnished?"

Marco nods an affirmative. "He sleeps there sometimes, if it's been a longer day. They have us clean it the next morning."

"Sounds like all we need is a little leak at the condo."

Miss Belle chuckles at Missa's words. "Okay, that'll be step four. Two days before sound good?"

"Yeah." Missa grins. "Let's give it time to get nice and flooded."

Beside her, Auntie shakes her head with a soft laugh.

Present

Buccero is here. The list of meetings he has on the books for each day of the week is extensive. He's barely had time to wine and dine government officials he's been so busy. Catching up on three years of prison time. Add on a flooded condo, and he's spent the last two nights sleeping in his fully furnished apartments at the top floor of his building.

My mouth goes dry as I step out of the elevator. My gun is drawn, held at my side with the safety off. My trigger finger rests along the barrel.

I suck in a breath and let it out slowly.

First is a foyer of sorts. A gap between the elevator and stairs, and the actual rooms that take up over half of the top floor. The other half is a rooftop pool and helo-pad.

Coats hang from hooks to the left of the door before me. A shallow bowl is set out on a tall table to the right, for keys and mail. An opaque square of glass set into the top half of the door shows a light on inside.

Something stirs in my gut. The villa was so protected. More guards than I accounted for, and Lydia. Our intel suggests she stayed in Arequipa, keeping an eye on the villa in case of another attack but...

"Fuck."

My free hand flies to my ear at my sister's voice. I dart down the hall a few feet, getting close to the stairs and away from the door to the apartments.

"Carmen? What's wrong?"

"They had... shit."

Her com goes quiet.

"Carmen?"

I'm at the stairs, pushing the door open as quietly as I can, letting it close, and then taking the stairs three at a time.

A thud comes across the com. A shout.

Louis's voice comes through. *"We have more guards incoming. I don't know where they came from. They aren't with the company."*

The blood freezes in my chest.

"Carmen?!" I hiss. "Answer me, damnit."

"Give me a—fuck." Scuffling. Another shout. A gunshot.

I kick through the door to the 42nd floor.

The stillness surprises me. The floor is dark. No lights from that far corner office, though city light coming in through the large glass windows shows a shadow of an open door.

I crouch. "Carmen, where the hell are you?" My voice is too quiet to carry through the room, but she'll hear me on the coms.

"Damen?" The split second of relief vanishes as quickly as it appeared. It's Miss Belle.

"What is going on?" I demand. I've slipped into Spanish. Too much fear is in my gut. "I don't see Carmen and she's not answering the coms."

"We think she's hiding, off the coms. Damen..." The hesitation drives a rush of terror through my chest. *"Lydia was waiting in Buccero's office."*

"I'm on that floor right now," I say. "There's no one here."

"She must have gone somewhere else then. Missa is still working on getting the cameras back up. Louis is out."

I move across the floor, sliding around desks and fake potted plants. The carpet beneath my feet is silent. Then it's not. I step in something wet. Sticky.

I crouch, knee to the ground. Dip my gloved fingers into a pool of dark liquid. Hold it up to the light coming in from outside... it's red.

"What do we do?" My hands shake. I stand and clench them into fists.

"This is your mission, Damen. You make the call."

I hesitate, and in that moment, static comes across the coms again.

Carmen's voice floods me with relief so intense I have to lean up against the wall to Buccero's private office to keep from collapsing.

"I'm here." She's panting, breathless. *"I'm fine. Had to run. I'm at the bottom of the elevator shaft, in the parking garage. I should be able to climb up and get out through the front but..."* There is a long pause. She swallows and I can hear the tears in her voice. *"Damen, I didn't get the info. That bitch was waiting for us. I can try to climb back up but... there are a dozen mercs crawling the building."*

My throat catches. I lean my head against the wall behind me, clenching my jaw so tight it hurts.

Miss Belle comes on again. *"Damen. This is your choice. The clock is ticking."*

My heart aches. Like a hot blade is piercing through my chest. Anxiety claws at my stomach.

One Week Ago

"Intel has to be the priority." Auntie's arms are crossed over her chest.

Carmen nods beside me, her expression twisted into a furious snarl.

Word just came in via one of Auntie's men still in the mountains. Protestors found three bodies. Villagers from the village that was bulldozed a few days before I flew to Peru.

Carmen had hoped they got out. Most of the villagers fled when Buccero's hired guns threatened to start shooting. It appears not everyone escaped in time.

Or maybe they stayed to try and stop the destruction. Either way, they're dead. Killed because of Buccero's greed, and the greed of the people he is working with.

I dip my head in a shallow nod. Heat has replaced some of the feeling in my limbs. Intel is one priority. Carmen's priority.

Ending Buccero is mine.

Present

The door to Buccero's private office is a few feet to my left. Once inside, all I need to do is boot up the computer and plug in the USB Missa gave me. It will take maybe two minutes.

I look back the way I came. Back to the stairwell, the elevator. The way to Buccero. He was already on guard. Already waiting for this to happen. Who knows how long Lydia has been staking out his office, ready for me to show up.

Who knows where he will go now, after a second attempt on his life.

He'll disappear.

The destruction his company is doing to the Amazon, to the native Peruvians living in the mountains there... that won't disappear.

"Get Carmen to the van." My voice trembles as I step away from the wall and through the open door to the office.

"Damen..."

"Get out of here, Carmen," I growl through gritted teeth. "I'll be down in five."

I power up the computer and the monitor, leaving the screen on just long enough to make sure the USB is working. Then I shut off the light and duck behind the desk.

Less than a minute later, the elevator dings and footsteps clomp across the ground toward me. I scoot back, getting into that space under the desk where the chair scoots in. My gun is out again, ready. I press my free hand to the cross under my shirt.

A pair of mercs don't bother to be quiet as they move through the floor.

"Why would she come back here?" one demands.

"Every floor means every floor. Suck it up and look."

A grumble, a kick of some piece of furniture that clatters to the ground. Only two of them, from the footsteps and voices. They do a slap-dash job of searching. One paces through the office, but there's no hesitation in their stride. No move to pull out the chair, check my hiding place.

I wait, barely breathing.

They take the stairs when they're done, one saying something about getting to the boss. I slide the chair out, turn on the monitor to double check 100% download, pull out the USB, and make for the stairs. Echoing slams of boots against the metal stairs reverberate through the stairwell. I shut the door and cross to the elevator.

I stand to the side, gun out and ready as the light reads 42 and the bell dings. The box is empty. I step inside, face the door, and hesitate as my finger reaches for the buttons.

My heart pounds.

Buccero has at least two men with him. Probably more. Lydia is likely there too. Are they waiting? Or has he fled?

Did he leave the moment someone was spotted in the building?

The bloody tip of my glove jams the L button. My hands shake as the elevator whooshes down. The USB drive in my interior vest pocket weighs heavy against my chest.

At the 20th floor, the elevator slows. I dart to the side, switching the gun for a blade in this enclosed space. A ding. The doors open. Two men step through, mid-conversation. They're both wearing the usual gear for a privately hired security squad. They turn. Both see me at the same time.

One hesitates. The other lunges. My blade, held at my side to conceal its existence, sinks into his gut. I shove him out the doors and jam the close button. The other goes for his gun. I kick. My boot crunches down on the bone just above his knee. He folds, then comes up swinging. I block and catch his other fist in my stomach.

The air flees my chest. I stagger back. Inhale. The doors start to close. I shove him back with an elbow. In the inches left between metal, the other man is rising from the ground, eyes widen as he sees the doors close. He rushes. Too late.

Another blow to the back of my neck. I turn. My blade is visible now. My grip shifts so the edge of the knife runs along my forearm.

We trade hits. I land more than he does, each one with my right hand leaves a slice in his skin or uniform. I kick his sternum, and he doubles over. We're at the 6th floor. I throw my elbow into the back of his neck, falling on him and knocking him to the ground. He's stunned. Conscious but dazed.

I shove the blade into my belt and pull zip ties from a pocket. Two around his hands, behind his back. He focuses up when I go for his ankles, kicking and cursing at me. He has a com device around his neck. More security will be on the way.

I punch him in the head, and he goes quiet for a few brief seconds. I get the ties secured around his ankles. Then I rip his sleeve and tie the fabric tight around his mouth. He can still make noise, but the gag pulls at his cheeks and stuffs his tongue down, keeping him from giving specific information.

Still, I have to move.

I stand, square up with my gun out again, and do a little back and forth on the balls of my feet.

"Are you ready for me?" I murmur.

"Carmen is with Auntie. We can be at the doors in seconds."

"Seconds are all I'm gonna have."

The elevator dings. The doors open. I run.

Chapter Nineteen

Miss Belle

It Got Fucked Up

Damen sprints toward me. I lean to the side, giving him room to dive into the van just as Missa hits the gas. Men pile out of the office building behind him. Some run forward. One manages to slap the side of the van before he stumbles off the sidewalk. I yank the door closed as gunshots start. Bullets pelt into the back of the van. Most are stopped by the 3-inch-thick planks of wood we installed yesterday. I duck as a few rip between the seams.

Missa is cursing. I come back up, flying into the side bench as we take a tight turn. I stifle a yelp as my hip slams into the wood.

"Are you okay?" I demand as I stick my head between the two front seats.

"Fine," she says through clenched teeth. "Let me drive."

I back away without a word.

Turning, I find Damen on the floor of the van, leaned against a bench. I hurry to him, unsteady on the rocking surface.

"Hey." I crouch. Scan his body for bullet holes or knife wounds. My survey stops when I catch sight of his expression.

He's not hurt.

"He's gone." Damen rips off his gloves, throwing them against the back. He runs his hand through his hair, shaking his head. "He's gone now. We won't get another chance like this."

I swallow and lick my dry lips. My stomach aches at the pain in his eyes. Now isn't the time to tell him he's wrong. It's not the time for half-truths and high hopes.

Instead, I lean against the bench next to him, my feet planted on the floor in an attempt to keep from shifting too much. I stare at the door across from us. Through the front windshield, flickering red and blue lights pass us by. Sirens, headed past us, back toward the business district.

We sit. The sounds of the city at night, rumbling traffic, and Missa's occasional mumbled curse are all that break the silence. Almost an hour passes before we hit gravel. The van slows to a stop. Missa steps out; the front door slams shut.

A long moment goes by.

"We should go check on Carmen," I say.

Damen nods, lips pursed tight together. He still doesn't move.

I push myself off the floor, holding back a groan as my stiff joints proclaim their displeasure. I slide open the door and limp out. A stretch helps. I suck in a breath, exhale, and turn to face the house. Rosie stands under the porch light, watching us with wide eyes. The other van hasn't arrived yet.

I glance at Missa, standing at the edge of the lane with her gaze fixed on the main road.

"Weren't they ahead of us?" I murmur as I move to stand beside her.

"Auntie took a longer route to get back."

I nod and return to the van. Damen sits on the edge, feet resting on the gravel, arms on his legs with his head down.

"No one got stabbed this time," I say, trying to inject some levity into my voice. I don't think I succeed.

Damen raises his head and glares at me. His eyes are red, tear streaks marking his face. He sniffs. Catches sight of Rosie.

His jaw is tight as he stands and moves past me. I stay where I am as he goes to his baby sister and pulls her into a hug. She asks about Carmen. He tells her they should be here soon. She doesn't ask if he did it. The failure of the whole thing is etched across his face.

A few more minutes go by. Rosie slinks back into the house at some point. She doesn't look at me. Hasn't in two days. My hands are still bruised.

Damen goes to stand with Missa. I sink onto the front porch steps.

Tires hit gravel. My gaze flicks up, and I watch Auntie's van rumble up the driveway. She pulls in next to the bullet-riddled vehicle and flies from her seat. In the time it takes me to stand, she has jerked open the back door and practically lifted Carmen out.

"I'm fine," Carmen insists in Spanish. She winces. Her pant leg is matted with blood.

"An elevator shaft?" Auntie demands. Her black braid shakes back and forth with her indignation. "What were you thinking?"

I arrive next to the two women at the same time Damen and Missa do. Carmen looks at her brother and swallows.

"I'm sorry. I didn't..." A pained grimace crosses her face.

"Let's get you inside," Auntie says.

Missa nods and moves in to put Carmen's arm around her shoulder. The girl limps toward the house, the women on either side helping to hold her up. She glances back at Damen, regret sunken into her eyes.

It's just Damen and me. Standing in the dark. In the cold. I watch him.

"It's not..." He sighs, his hand running through his hair again. "I know it's not her fault."

He finally meets my eye. I nod. "Make sure she knows it. When things go wrong like this, it's easy to sink into guilt. Make sure she knows."

He bites his lower lip, sucks in a breath, and strides to the house.

I look up. The stars are bright here. Even with the light from the front porch. We're close to the ocean. Close to the horizon line that doesn't falter, doesn't lift or sink. Just sits.

I pace around the side of the house toward the cliffs. I need a glimpse of that horizon. Just for a minute. To ease the anxiety crawling through my gut like worms.

It's all dark. The sea, the sky. There is no line for me to look at this late at night. Even the stars don't clarify it, their light reflected so perfectly on the ocean's surface.

The anxiety lifts to my chest. It tightens. Grips like a vice. Closes in, and I can't breathe. I can't....

My fist is closed. I press it against my chest and rub. I can scrub this way.

I swallow. The dark of the sky and sea closes in. I force down a breath and press harder. My hands are shaking. Hands, legs... I sink to my knees in the tall waving grass. My vision blurs for a moment. The stars dim.

I don't know how long I sit there. On my knees, drawing my hand across my chest so hard I open the scabs on my knuckles.

A voice startles me out of my daze, stupor, whatever you'd call it.

I blink a few times, the pressure receding. I gasp, the shallow breaths I'd been drawing not nearly enough to fill my lungs.

Someone touches my shoulder.

I jerk to the side, rolling through the grass and come up to my knees, fists raised.

Missa stands before me, her gaze wide. Her hand is out. She's the one who touched me. Her fingers are the ones I flinched away from.

Cold floods me.

"Belle…"

I clear my throat, shaking. "Yeah. I know."

Her expression shifts. Changing from alarm to something sad. Something understanding.

Something that widens the cracks in my heart.

"We should go in." Missa gestures toward the house. "It's cold out here."

"I don't feel it," I mumble.

She sinks onto the grass next to me. Her movements are slow—like I'm some kind of wounded animal. Maybe I am.

"Carmen is going to be all right."

I nod.

"The leg isn't broken. Twisted, and slashed pretty good. She has decent bruising on her face. But she took on Lydia and won. We won't know if that bitch survived until Buccero's people do a press release."

"Carmen was the one who took the shot." It's not a question, but Missa answers it like one.

"Yeah. She pulled the gun as soon as Lydia showed her face. Got her in the shoulder. Their fight happened after. Lydia lost a lot of blood."

"Did Carmen get the gun out?"

Missa nods, her gaze fixed on the lack of horizon. "Didn't bleed on anything either. She stopped up the wounds with spare cloth while she was hiding."

I pull my knees up, elbows latched around them as I pick at my fingernails. "Auntie taught her well."

"A different style," Missa murmurs, "but I like it."

"Maybe we can get her to do a guest lesson for the Guides."

We are both silent for a while. Waves crash against the rocks. Far enough that the sound is muffled. Muted. Background noise like you'd use to put an infant to sleep.

I want to sleep. God, do I want to sleep. A dreamless night for once. Just me and the black of my eyelids.

"I'm so tired."

My voice breaks, and I hate it. I hate that I'm like this. Hate that the mission went so sideways. Hate that I didn't anticipate Lydia lying in wait. Hate the pain Damen is in. Hate that Missa is right.

Missa is right.

"You're right."

She scoots closer, still not saying a word. Her shoulders are higher than mine, her torso taller. It feels so natural to lean my head against her. There is no squish to her, but it's still comfortable. Comforting. Flashes me back to high school, long nights studying, watching old movies, eating too much popcorn, and crying about boys.

I don't think the me back then would recognize the me now. I don't think she'd like me. I think I'd like her.

I'm not sure how long we sit out here. At some point, I notice Missa shivering, and I pull myself together enough to rise and get inside.

The remains of our mission are scattered across the kitchen table. Weapons, supplies, and in the center—spaced out from the rest—a small black thumb drive.

I look at Missa as she flips the lock on the back door. "He got it?"

She nods. "He got it."

I exhale what feels like a chestful of ice. Warmth begins to seep back into my lungs, though my fingers are frozen stiff.

"Let's get to bed," Missa murmurs. "We can work on damage control in the morning."

For once, I listen.

Chapter Twenty

Miss Belle

Like a Moth to Flame

The morning comes too soon, but not soon enough. My dreams are plagued by blood. Lifeless eyes staring at me. Bodies beyond count—which is definitely my brain's way of getting me to seek help since I haven't killed too many people to count.

I count them all the time.

Not on purpose. Just something that happens when my mind gets too quiet.

I dress quickly, lurching downstairs to get back into a hustle and bustle. Back to noise.

Carmen sits on the couch next to Rosie. The younger sister is applying a fresh set of bandages across Carmen's arm. Clean lines—from a blade—mar her skin. They dribble blood, but not enough to be concerned about.

Carmen catches my eye as I walk through to the kitchen. She nods, but there's something in her gaze. I recognize guilt.

Damen may have already spoken to her, but I need to as well. I should find out if Auntie talked to her yet.

Missa looks up when I step into the kitchen. She strides into the room, pushes a hot bowl of oatmeal into my hands, and jerks her head at the table. Damen is sitting there, staring at the small TV on the far counter. His hands clench a steaming mug of fresh coffee.

Adjacent to him, Auntie is poring over a thick Lenovo Legion 5 laptop—top of the line for this kind of work, the little black thumb drive sticking out the side.

I settle into the chair across from her, corner seat to Damen. I'm not blocking his view, but he leans away when I set my bowl down.

I open my mouth, hesitate, and turn to watch the screen as well.

Letters flash across the TV, announcing a breaking news broadcast. More information about the "Buccero Break-In."

What a clever name.

A journalist appears, sitting comfortably behind a dull yellow desk, and straightens his tie. I pick up my spoon and begin shoveling breakfast into my mouth, ears perked up and concentrating on the rapid Spanish coming from the TV.

They're calling it a break-in rather than an attempted murder. Blaming old rumors about Buccero. Painting him as a victim of fake news and bigotry. Buttering up sympathy for a poor man trying to get back on his feet, trying to turn his life around after a stint in prison for tax fraud.

Heat comes off Damen in waves. He hasn't lifted his drink once, his knuckles white around the mug, jaw clenched like a vice. He's shaking.

When the screen shifts from the news station to a reporter at the front of the building I look up again. They talk about the head of security. Injured. In critical care at a local hospital.

A grin slides up the side of my face as the woman on the screen laments that Lydia might not survive until tomorrow.

"Remind me to buy your sister something nice," I murmur.

Damen growls. "They're making him a victim," he utters through clenched teeth.

Auntie and I exchange a look over her computer for a brief second.

"Give Auntie a few days to get the information to the right channels, and they won't look at him as anything but a villain again."

"The only place they should be looking at him is in a *casket*."

The bitterness in his voice shoots a burst of caution through me. A warning.

"Hey," I put a hand on his arm, "we *will* come back, Damen. But there's a shit-storm of media on this, and it's only going to get worse. Not to mention the people Buccero has on him. He knew we were after him the moment they realized someone was in the building. It's too hot right now. We need to lay low for a few days, get out of the country, and try again when things cool down."

Damen pushes back from the table, gives me a look that burns into my soul, and storms away.

I stand up, cross to the television, and shut it off. My hands are trembling as I lean against the counter and fold my arms.

At the table, Auntie clears her throat.

I meet her gaze again.

"He is going to do something dangerous unless someone stops him."

I nod, jaw tight. "Is it what you need? The information he got?"

She breathes in deep, clicks her tongue, and raises her eyebrows. "It's what I need. It's more than what I need." She hits a few buttons and closes the laptop. The laugh lines on her face crease as a smile crosses her lips. "It's enough to permanently destroy the company. I don't care how many millionaires he has in his pocket, or how many Americans are working with him, he can't recover from this."

"Good," I mumble.

The next two days pass in a blur. Auntie delivers her information, but it will take some time for things to fall into place. For Buccero to get the ending he deserves.

Missa watches me. I watch Damen. He sits in front of his sister's laptop, rewatching countless interviews with Buccero's young assistant. He barely eats. I catch him sometimes staring at the blueprints again. I remind him we will come back.

He doesn't believe me.

Missa has stopped pestering me about Doc. I imagine it's because our in-house psychiatrist told her I called to make an appointment. Next week. After we get back to the states. After I have time to figure out some of this cop stuff we are dealing with.

Missa also makes a call to that asshole who works in the Commissioner's office. She's going on that third date. Something tells me it's her way of bribing me into going to therapy. Not that she needs to. Not after seeing Rosie's face. The way her gaze sticks on my bruised knuckles when she thinks I'm not watching.

I spend a lot of time on the cliffs. Sitting and watching the sea.

We purchase plane tickets. Make sure Auntie's men get home safe. Maria and Rosie are going back to Arequipa. Carmen and Auntie will head to Cuzco—and travel to the villages further northeast when they land. Damen, Missa, and I are all going back to New York.

Something is still nagging at the back of my mind when I hand over Damen's ticket. "Hey." A piece falls into place. "Did you get a chance to buy that painting you wanted to get from my sister?"

Damen pauses, his fingers clutching the edge of the ticket. He meets my eye. There's something there. Something in the slight flinch of his cheek...

"Uh, I bought it, and another. But I haven't had them picked up yet if that's what you're asking."

"Right," I murmur. My brain whirs, heating up as it tries to fit the puzzle piece of what I'm missing into place.

"I was planning on going back to Brooklyn for another couple weeks, if that's all right with you," Damen says.

There it is again, something in his voice this time. I stare at the wall behind him, lips pursed as I jut my jaw to the side, concentrating. My head isn't working as quickly as I'm used to.

Damen's room floats into my mind. The four-star hotel room I pay for each time he goes to Brooklyn... empty. Un-lived in.

My sister's words about the paintings. About the art collector from Europe.

I watch him watch me make the connection. As my eyes narrow, his widen. My hands ball into fists, and his spread in a defensive gesture.

"Damen," I growl, taking a step forward.

The room around us has gone silent. Auntie and Carmen, previously chatting at the table, now watch as I step again, vibrating with anger. Missa moves around them. Not stepping between Damen and me but getting herself closer.

"Miss Belle," he replies weakly.

This is how I know. How I become entirely sure in the space of a second. Because Damen has been cold and short with me since our failure to execute his abuser. But now...

"Are you sleeping with my sister?" I demand through clenched teeth.

He swallows. Heat rushes me, and I slam him against the wall. My forearm is pressed against his neck, my face inches from his, my breathing heavy.

His hands are still raised in that defensive gesture. "I'm not... Miss Belle, it's more complicated than that."

"More complicated?" I repeat, my voice quieting to a hiss of steaming rage. "How? Explain it to me, Damen. Explain how you're fucking my little sister behind my back. Explain how it's complicated."

Someone behind me sucks in air. I ignore it.

"It's not... it's not like that."

"Not like *what*?" I snap.

"Belle," Missa interrupts.

I hesitate, my gaze flicking to her for a brief second. She raises an eyebrow, and I note the edge of a smile on her lips. It sends another flash of angry heat through me.

I turn back to Damen and release my hold. He sinks a bit as his feet find purchase on the floor. I didn't realize I'd pushed him up so much.

I wheel around and pace across the kitchen and back. Damen doesn't move.

I glare at him. "If you and my sister are having fun having sex, fine. She's an adult; you're one too. I'll be bitchy about you keeping it a secret. But *fine*. But..." I move toward him again, and he backs into the wall again. "If you're in a *relationship* with her? If you've told her the truth about us. About me..." My breathing gets heavy, and I swear I see spots for a second.

He gives the slightest shake of his head.

"Worse," I cut off any words he might be about to say, my teeth clenched. "If she's in love with you, and you're lying to her..." I tilt my head, a warning. A threat.

He swallows. "I don't... I don't know what we are right now."

A chill runs down my spine. "But you are something?"

He gives a small nod.

"Does she know?"

He shakes his head.

I storm out of the room.

Chapter Twenty-One

Damen

A Murder

Talking to Auntie was easy. Talking to Miss Belle was harder. After everything with Em... she has every right to be furious with me. She still helped.

Helped because I promised not to do this yet. I promised to wait.

I press my crucifix to my lips. Saints have lied; God will forgive me.

I breathe in slowly. Through the nose, out my mouth. Silent. Quiet in the dark.

Mama and Rosie should be getting to Arequipa right now. I was supposed to be on that flight. Told Missa I wanted some time with them before heading back to New York. If this goes right, I'll arrive in the States a little after she and Miss Belle get back, on the connecting flight they booked me out of Lima.

If this goes right.

A door opens in the room. I'm tucked away, hiding in this tiny coat closet. Footsteps pad across the carpet. Someone murmurs, barely distinguishable words as they pace the office.

It's not Buccero.

I flex my fingers around the grip of my gun.

The young voice of Arturo, so familiar to me after watching countless interviews given by Buccero's assistant, brings hesitation to my plans. He wasn't supposed to be here today.

No one was. No one but Buccero. After the news hit, his company tanked. The same reporters lauding his bravery after the break-in were calling him a pig barely three days later. Over a thousand people lost their jobs. The government seized a handful of properties. This building is the last of Buccero's legacy.

I catch a few of his words as he walks past the closet. "... *have* to do this. You can do this."

He sounds terrified.

I grit my teeth. This was already a longshot. A dangerous idea that may get me killed and will definitely get me fired from the Guides.

And now there's an extra complication.

I wait for his footsteps to walk away from my hiding spot, then I crack the door.

Arturo is dressed impeccably, his suit pressed and clean, shoes polished, hair slicked down with plenty of gel.

He's holding a gun.

My heart sinks, and I step out of the closet.

Arturo turns at the far end of the spacious office, still smelling faintly of bleach from the cleaning crew getting rid of Lydia's blood on the carpet.

He spots me and gasps. He raises the gun, his finger already on the trigger.

"Wait." I hold up my hands, my own weapon dangling from a finger as I have no intention of setting it down. "I'm not here to hurt you, Arturo."

His hand trembles. A burst of fear goes through me at the thought of being accidentally killed by this boy before Buccero arrives.

"You..." Arturo takes a step closer, his gun lowering a few inches. "I've seen you before."

I nod. "At Buccero's villa."

He swallows. "Lydia had you."

I nod again, offering a tight smile. "She thought she did." I slowly return my hands to my sides, holstering the gun as he watches me with wary, wide, eyes.

"You were his assistant, years ago." Arturo's arms fall to his sides. I nearly flinch at the carelessness with which he handles his weapon.

"Yeah."

His lips tremble, fear and shame flashing through his eyes. "Did he..."

"Yeah." My stomach clenches with a fresh wave of guilt. The chain of my necklace feels heavy against the back of my neck. I take a step toward him. "I tried to end it, Arturo. I..." I lick my lips as heat floods my limbs. "I thought I stopped him."

A burst of anger splits through the doe-eyed expression on the boy's face. "You didn't though. You didn't stop him."

I sigh, my eyes burning with tears that can't fall right now. "I'm sorry."

"You're the one who was here last week?"

I glance at the door, a worrying thought occurring to me that maybe this is a set up. Maybe Arturo is wearing a wire. Maybe I'm about to be ambushed by hired goons.

Arturo takes a step toward me, the earnest look in his eye driving a spike through my chest. "You know Lydia is dead?"

I can't help the twitch at the edge of my mouth. God will forgive that too. "Yes."

Tears fill Arturo's eyes. "Why didn't you kill him?"

It feels like the floor has fallen out from under me. My hands clench into fists at my sides, and I grit my teeth. "I wanted to, Arturo. But there were more important things to be done—"

"More important?" Arturo hisses, pain lacing his words.

My jaw is so tight the muscles in my neck are aching. "More important," I confirm. "Because they were to stop everything he's doing along the Amazon. I was so close but..." I break off with a grimace.

Then my ears pick up a familiar sound. Footsteps, padding across the carpet beyond the door. I take two steps back, my hand jumps to my gun, and the door opens.

The blood in my veins runs cold at how hale and healthy Buccero is up close. His time in prison was not the punishment I'd imagined. Or maybe he's stuffed himself at every meal since getting out. It's hard to say.

His suit is pressed and clean, his thinning hair slicked back with gel, a small scar on his jawline from a snowboarding accident in his youth.

He looks just as I remember in my nightmares.

Well, except for the surprise plastered across his expression.

"Arturo?" Buccero sees him first, his beady gaze taking in the gun in his assistant's hand. Then his eyes meet mine.

Just behind him, a burly man strides through the door. His weapon is already drawn, loose at his side.

I curse not keeping mine out while talking to Arturo.

Buccero's leg twitches, like he's going to take a step back, but he shifts, widening his stance and looking back and forth from me to the boy.

"*Jefe?*" His security guard moves through the room. Hulking and massive, he takes a position a bit to the side of Buccero. Though Arturo is the one with a gun in hand, the ape-ish man keeps his gaze on me.

"It's all right," Buccero chuckles. He looked to his assistant. "Excellent work, Arturo. I see you've detained an intruder."

A flare of rage so intense it sends sparks across my eyes blinds me for a brief second. "Not quite, Vincente."

The bastard doesn't look at me. He keeps his gaze on Arturo. "What lies has he told you, Arty, my boy?"

Arturo's hand trembles. The gun is at his side. Tears well in his eyes again.

"No lies," I growl. "Not anymore."

"I'm not addressing *you*," he snaps.

I don't flinch. Arturo does. He raises his gun, pointing it, shaking, in Buccero's direction. The hired goon takes another step toward Arturo, his weapon now pointed at the boy's chest.

Buccero puts up a hand and lowers his voice. "No need for that, Arty. Whatever this man has told you, you do not work for him. You work for me. We take care of each other."

"You don't take care of him." I take a step. "You use him. Just like you've always used everyone around you. It ends now, Vincente. Your company is in ruins. The media has turned on you. The feds will close in on you soon enough. You're done."

This fractures Buccero's smooth demeanor again. A deep scowl creases his face. "How dare you. You've tried this before, Damen. It won't last."

"This will." Arturo's voice shakes as he tightens his grip on the little pistol in his hands.

The gorilla aims for the boy.

My gun is in my hand before all of my mind registers that I drew it. A shot fires off, deafening in the enclosed space of the office.

The hired security lurches. The weapon falls from his hand and thunks on the carpet. He staggers to the side, clutching his chest. He falls and goes still.

Now Buccero has fear in his eyes. "Arturo, what are you doing?" he snaps. "This man is not worth throwing your life away. He *killed* Lydia. He will kill you too, just to get to me."

Arturo shakes his head, tears streaming down his cheeks. "I can't do this anymore, Señor. I can't..."

I step between them.

Arturo's desperate intake of air behind me sends a brief snap of fear into my spine. His gun is to my back now, mine leveled at our abuser.

"No more," I murmur. I meet Buccero's gaze.

I've seen this man in every situation, from negotiating deals with cartels, to dancing with pretty women at galas. I've watched him wiggle his way out of deadly situations, and artfully threaten a man enough to make him piss himself.

Never have I seen defeat in his eyes. Not even when his verdict was placed, and he was sent to prison three years ago.

But I see it there now.

Something releases within me. Warmth caresses me. This must be what an epiphany feels like. A solidifying, concrete sense of purpose melts the ice around my heart. I thought I needed it, needed to protect myself from what I'm about to do.

I don't.

Time seems to slow as I let myself absorb every second. Arturo lets out a choked sob behind me. My heart beats.

Buccero shakes his head, a gelled streak of hair flopping out of place.

I inhale.

My finger squeezes, ever so gently, against the trigger.

Time returns to normal as the bullet exits the chamber and buries itself in Buccero's chest. He is dead by the time his body hits the carpet.

Arturo gasps. He wheels, vomiting into a trash bin beside the desk.

Calm fills me. My heartbeat is steady.

I give my gun a moment to cool, then holster it and turn to the boy. "I think it's time to get out of here, Arturo."

He wipes the back of his hand across his mouth. "What... what do I do? What do I do now?"

The shock is intense. His eyes are as wide as if he'd just taken a tab of acid. He glances down at Buccero as I guide him from the office and makes a retching sound again.

But he holds it down. We cross to the elevator, and he leans on me a little as we wait. The bell dings, the box opens, and we step inside.

I poke a gloved finger at the garage floor button.

"What did we do?" Arturo asks between almost hyperventilating breaths.

I cut a glance his way. He's sweaty and shaking. "*We* didn't do anything." I pause, mulling over how much I sound like

Miss Belle in this moment. "*I* took care of something that never should have been on your shoulders. I'm sorry, Arturo. If I'd done that three years ago—"

He trembles, shaking his head as his wide eyes meet mine. "I don't... I don't know where to go now."

My lips part as somehow this is the moment my nerves decide to reappear.

"Are you... do you have family around?"

Arturo swallows. "I have my *tias*, in Aguas Calientes."

I nod. "I can get you there, Arturo."

He sniffs. "I... thank you. I don't even know your name."

I chuckle, feeling lighter than I have in months. "You don't need to."

The elevator dings, and we step into the parking garage under the building.

CHAPTER TWENTY-TWO

MISS BELLE

THE CIRCLE WIDENS

I nurse a beer, my grip loose on the bottle, my mind happily fuzzy. Well, not happily, but it's nice to let things go for a little bit. Even if it's only until I land in New York.

Once I get on whatever kind of meds Doc suggests—which is almost a guarantee given the number of panic attacks I've had on this trip—I won't be drinking at all. I don't much anyway; it's not a huge deal, but having this last one feels right.

It's helping my stress, even temporarily.

Rosie came to me before we left, as Carmen and Maria were loading up the rental car and finalizing plans with Auntie. Damen's little sister, the sweet girl who wants to be a nurse, handed me a cookie, gave me a soft hug, and murmured thank you.

It nearly broke me right then and there.

Missa confirmed my appointment with Doc on our way to the airport in Lima. I meet with her in two days.

For now, I glance at the TV hanging in the corner and ask the bartender to turn it up. Beside me, Auntie nods in agreement. She brings her glass bottle to her lips, takes a swig, and points at the screen.

"Interesting technique there, using the ID card to go in that way."

I grin, stretching my neck as the newscaster goes into detail about the case. "That move on the staircase was impressive."

She shrugs one shoulder. "It would have been better if the cameras had been entirely disabled."

"Agreed." I cock my head at the screen where a blurry still from security footage pops up. "But I don't think it'll be an issue given the equipment on hand."

Auntie chuckles. "You certainly know how to pack, Miss Belle."

I raise my bottle in a salute. "And you know how to plan."

She salutes back, and we fall into comfortable silence for a few minutes. The news station throws up some pictures of Vincente Buccero. Him graduating University, shaking hands with the previous president, getting sentenced, wearing a prison jumpsuit, and getting out. The photo they'll use at his funeral. *The rise and fall of one of the biggest con men in Peru's history,* is what the screen says.

I snort. "Fall is right."

Auntie shakes her head. "I wish I could have been there. The rumors... Carmen said they were true? I didn't want to ask before..."

I nod, my jaw clenching for a few seconds. "They're true. I thought it was handled before but—" I pause as the newscaster reiterates that the police have no suspects in custody and limited leads.

"Perhaps it was better this way." Auntie scoots her empty bottle across the bar. The bartender walks by, plopping another one in front of her as he heads toward a couple further down. "The company went first. I do not believe law enforcement will try very hard to solve this one. Not knowing the truth of what Buccero was doing to our country and our people."

I suck in a breath through my lips and let it out in a long exhale. "Yeah. That's the hope, right? That little fucker better get on a flight soon though."

She chuckles again, a deep throaty sound of someone who has spent a long time barking orders. "You truly didn't know he was going to do it?"

It's my turn to shrug. "I don't know, Auntie. Maybe I'm getting too old for this game."

She slaps a hand on my shoulder, making me flinch. "You're half my age, Miss Belle. Don't start that. You knew what was coming when he asked for your help. You gave it because it was the right thing to do."

"And because that bitch, Lydia, was dead."

She cracks a grin and nods. "It helps knowing that particular evil is no longer in this world."

We clink our bottles. Missa returns from the bathroom. She detoured somewhere along the way and plants a stick of Peruvian chocolate onto the bar top.

I raise an eyebrow at her.

She shrugs. "You'll probably have to do no sugar for a bit too."

My groan is drowned out by Auntie's cackle.

"I'm envious," she says with a smile at Missa. "If I'd had more women like you around in my youth..."

My cheeks flush, but Missa takes the complement in stride and thanks her for us both.

It's not much longer before Auntie's flight leaves. She departs with a promise to reach out if she ever needs our skillset and a friendly order for us to do the same.

Missa and I still have a while to wait.

"My date is in a week," Missa says with a scowl.

It takes me a minute to register her words. When it clicks, I glance her way with a grin. "Are you excited?"

"Oh fuck off," she grumbles. But there's a smile on her face. It shifts quickly to worry. "Do you know what you'll say to the Commissioner? Assuming I can get you a meeting?"

I shake my head, running a hand through my loose hair. Having my hair up has been giving me a headache; even a braid felt too constricting. "It depends on how much he knows. I need to make some calls and find out if he has contacts with some of the acronym agencies."

Her eyebrows nearly hit her hairline. "You're going to tell him the truth?"

I snort. "Well, part of the truth at least. I'm not sure how to smooth over the escort thing with a police commissioner without some kind of explanation about what's really going on."

Missa shakes her head. "The circle is growing, Belle."

I heave a sigh and stretch back in the uncomfortable airport chair. "Faster and faster, it seems." Pain flares in my ribs, less now than when we first arrived, but a reminder of the dangers of our work just the same.

"Next steps?"

"Take care of the cops. After that... I don't know. Maybe we scale down a bit, take a break after the summer."

"Is that even possible?"

I glance out the window ahead of us. A plane taxis down the airstrip, heading toward our gate. People will disembark. Flight attendants will do a quick clean. We will board, fly north, arrive in JFK and get back to the Manor. Then what? A few weeks of rest before we head to California for that stupid reunion? A summer of assignments that are guaranteed to drive my anxiety to the breaking point, trying to figure out what to do about Damen and my sister, contacting Lacey about her future with Miss Belle's Travel Guides...

It's too much.

I close my eyes, lean my head back, and slow my breathing. Missa runs her fingers through my hair for a bit.

Eventually, we get on the plane and head home.

Chapter Twenty-Three

Damen

Good at Secrets

I get Arturo safely to his *tias* in Aguas Calientes. Turns out his parents died just before he graduated. Just before Buccero hired him.

I was at least a few years into my grief about my father when I started the job. I can't imagine going through the grieving process while dealing with everything Buccero did to him.

Part of me is proud when we part. He doesn't have my name, and–according to new reports–the police looking into the murders of Buccero and his hired gun have no leads.

I even get a text from Auntie as I board the plane back to New York.

Nice work, kid. You and your sister are a lot alike. You have my number, if you ever need anything.

Missa texts too. A simple request for me to let her know when I've boarded. I'm going to be on a short leash for a long time.

But I don't mind. Good was done when that bullet ripped through Buccero's heart. I know this. I prayed on it during my trek back to New York.

Mama might not forgive me for a long time. But I don't think my relationship with God will face the same strain.

I call Em when the plane lands.

My phone is in my hand, my nearly numb legs taking me through the doors of LaGuardia, my mind tired and fuzzy from the events of the last couple weeks.

I'm bandaged and bloody and not looking forward to explaining the injuries to Em.

Miss Belle's final words to me, when she thought I was heading to the airport instead of to Buccero's offices, echo in my mind. *"Until I decide what to do, you say nothing. Clearly you're good at secrets; keep it that way."*

That was after she and I walked through different ways to kill Buccero. After I promised not to do anything until a few months had passed. After I told her I'd go back to New York like she wanted.

I am good at secrets.

But clearly so is she because Em is waiting for me outside.

I almost drop my phone. She grins from the sidewalk beside a taxi, offering a small wave as I hurry over.

"What are you—"

The smile on her face lights every nerve in my body. She cuts me off with a tight hug that pulls a pained groan from my lips.

"Your boss called," she laughs. "He said you'd be landing soon. It was a rough trip?"

I nod, my jaw somewhat slack as my mind catches up with her words. "Yeah... yeah, it was difficult seeing my family and..."

"Didn't get the piece you wanted?" Em loops her arm through mine, gently pulling me to the trunk so we can deposit my go-bag.

I don't answer for a moment. We climb into the back seat, and she leans against me—not the stabbed side, fortunately. I pull her close, pressing my lips to her forehead. "I got it, just took some work. And more time than I planned. I'm..." My heart thunders in my chest, furious at me for not being honest, and at the same time endlessly grateful to Miss Belle. I've disobeyed her enough to last a lifetime. "I'm sorry I was gone so long. I missed you."

As the taxi pulls into busy traffic, Em traces the curve of my jaw with her fingers. She doesn't ask about the bruises, though her eyebrow raises. Instead, she gives a gentle tug, pulling my face towards hers. Our lips lock, and the rush of heat drives every cold, distant, conflicted feeling from my body.

There are things to be done still. I want to help Carmen continue her work with the Quechua people in the mountains. I need to go by the church and talk with the Father. There are... many things to be addressed in confessional.

I want Em. As we dive deeper into the kiss, her lips like water after forty days of thirst in the desert, I realize just how much I want her.

I want her to know me. I want to live together, to meet her parents, to grow old with her.

A tingle runs down my spine. My fingers tangle in her hair. After a moment, she breaks away.

"I've missed you too. How long do you have this time?"

I hesitate, my brain catching up with the pause in the passion. "I think... I think as long as I want. I'll reach out to my boss when I'm ready for another assignment. But, until then, I'm..." I swallow. The crucifix presses, warm and reassuring, against my chest. "I'm yours, my love."

MISS BELLE'S
MB
TRAVEL GUIDES

ACKNOWLEDGEMENTS

Huge thanks to my beta readers; the lot of you are more help than you can imagine.

Tracey, this one is dedicated to you, but I also have to shout out your ability to design covers – for the entire series – as well as the peace of mind you bring with proofreading. I appreciate you so much.

Rachel, your help planning these books all those years ago are the reason they are happening now. Love you, Sissy.

Readers, thank you so much for continuing on Miss Belle's adventures. I am so excited for where this series is going, and I hope you are too.

Where to Find More

Hey friends! Head to chlyn.com to find my complete collection of works, sign up for my newsletter, and find out about upcoming in-person events!

Keep reading for a sneak peek of Delilah Goes to Chicago, releasing in 2025.

Delilah Goes to Chicago

Delilah

"Yeah, I've got this."

I don't got this. A shudder runs down my spine, the open side of the helicopter ahead of me, clouds below as though we've flown all the way to heaven and now my teacher wants me to jump back to hell.

Erin raises an eyebrow from her seat behind the pilot's chair. The neat brown strands don't quite match her flaming red hair, recently touched up in the bathroom while she gave me a tutorial in rapid disguise.

"You do," she says into the mic on her headset.

I exhale. I really don't got this. I've flown twice. From California to Tokyo, and Tokyo to Chicago. At least on the second one I had a hand to hold during take-off.

My thoughts drift away for a moment, caught on wondering when I'll get to see Lacey again. What mission she might be on for Miss Belle. If she's in danger. If she knows I chose to do this, to join their team.

The jump instructor's voice behind me reaches my ear. "Whenever you're ready."

My throat goes dry, but I tap her hand. She steps forward, me just a half-second off the timing. But the woman teaching me to skydive is sturdy, she keeps us up. We reach the door and I grab onto a thick nylon strap before stepping onto the helicopter's skit. My feet wobble on the rounded landing gear.

"When you let go, we jump. Remember to pull green when I tell you."

I nod, the helmet on my head flopping back and forth. I feel a burst of unexplainable humor. Why are we even wearing helmets? They won't help if the shoot doesn't open.

The laughter bubbling in my chest fizzes out. I open my mouth to say stop, raising my hand and...

The instructor steps.

I'm falling...

Falling...

Flying.

Abuelo help me, I might not hate this.

The sky opens below me. Green so far in the distance it feels like we won't make it there. We will simply fall forever.

Wind rips at my hair, my shirt, my skin. It's cold. Even with the layers of clothes required for this kind of thing.

"Pretty incredible, isn't it?" The woman behind me calls into my ear.

I nod. My jaw is too tight to open.

"Give it a count of ten, then pull," she says.

I close my eyes again, but the darkness is worse than seeing what we are careening towards.

Only five weeks into training, but Erin's words—the reason for stuff like this—echo in my head. We need to "practice everything" because you "never know."

Lesson #1: Danger is around every corner. Be prepared for anything.

I don't want to pull the shoot. Landing terrifies me.

The count ends. I pull the cord.

My hips and torso take the brunt of the stop as the parachute catches air and slows our descent.

This is somehow better and a million times worse. The view brings tears to my eyes, as does the wind and the desire to have my feet planted on solid earth again.

But then the ground is too close, and I'm running in the air like a cartoon, and we're landing.

Ouch.

My ankle twists under my weight and some of the instructor's weight. Damnit.

The pain is fleeting. A quick twist. Bruised but not broken.

"You okay?" Erin hurries to me as I yank off the gear.

I straighten, putting more weight on my left side than is wise, but she can't know I got hurt. "I'm fine. Good jump."

The instructor, a woman several inches taller than me with a long tight braid of blonde, nods with a smile. "It was. You did really well."

Good. She also didn't notice the twist. My ankle burns, the tender bruise unhappy with me putting a normal amount of weight on it.

"Thanks."

I can't say more than that. Can't get out enough words to offer up an actual thanks for the effort she's put into training me the past few days. It's been an intensive course in parachuting. Again—just in case.

"Home?" Erin's eyes are lined with black, lashes perfectly mascara'd with no chunks or pieces stuck together. A fain touch of brown highlights the blue pigments in her hazel eyes. "Or food first?"

She helps me organize my borrowed gear. We stow it aside for the parachuting team to put away when they go back to the launch area. By the time we walk back to her little black mini cooper, my ankle feels swollen in my shoe.

The thought of food pushes me through to the passenger seat. I lean against the plush leather and breathe through my nose. I could say something. Mention the pain, ask for ice, tell her I want to stay in and have a quiet evening.

But I can't.

I can't have her looking at me as though I need rescuing. And I certainly can't have her thinking I'm not up to the task of joining Miss Belle's Travel Guides. That wouldn't be fair anyway. It's only been five weeks.

My pulse quickens as this train of thought gets away from me.

Getting kicked out because of an injury—no. That can't happen. It won't.

Besides, it's just a twisted ankle. I'll elevate it when I go to bed. Elevate. One of those fancy words Erin had to explain the first time she used it.

I stare out the window as we hit traffic and my stomach grumbles.

"Tacos?"

My lip curls before I catch myself.

"Riiight," Erin says with a grin. "These aren't tacos."

"Can we do cheesesteak instead?"

The woman shifts into third as a section of traffic opens up. "Yeah, that sounds great."

I catch sight of a bright red bird perched on a wire. "Do we have lessons tonight?"

Erin's gaze snags on me for a brief moment before she faces the road again. "Not tonight, no. It's the off day. Why? Did you want to throw in some extra French practice?"

"Oh." I sink a little in my chair. "I can, if you wanted—"

"Kidding, Delilah. You can go see your little friend tonight."

I swallow, trying to keep the surprise from being so painfully clear on my face. Why can't I learn how to hide my emotions?

"Be careful, okay?" She glances at me again before making the turn to take us to the best food truck in Chicago. "I'm glad you took my advice to find friends in low places but watch your back when you're with them."

"I know," I murmur. "You don't have to worry about me over-trusting someone."

The bitter smile on her lips suggests she has been talking to Doc—the shrink I'm forced to talk to a few times a week as part of my training. So far it's been a whole lot of her telling me I've never done anything wrong in my life and I have many options outside of Miss Belle.

The last time we spoke she actually got me to open up about how I met Jose and got wrapped up in the life that came before Tokyo, before Lacey. But based on Erin's expression, I can't let my guard down again like that.

Those memories, those fears, won't get in the way of this training. This opportunity.

"I'm more concerned with a raid while you're at the club. But yeah, maybe also don't trust gang bangers to be the closest friends you make out here."

I huff a laugh through my nose. "Oh, I'm not. You're the closest friend I've made out here, Erin."

She doesn't reply, and the car gets very quiet. Despite the late spring afternoon sun, I feel suddenly cold.

I stay silent. My stomach clenches. What did I say? What did I do to earn the silent treatment? I twist a strand of black hair loose from my bun.

When we pull into the parking lot where this food truck crew makes their living, Erin pulls up the parking break and turns to face me head-on.

"I'm not your friend."

I mask, but I know my wince was visible. I shrug. "Right. But I can talk to you about stuff."

She presses her lips together, rolling them as though she's just applied gloss. "Yes. To an extent."

My thick eyebrows draw together. I don't bother to smooth the confusion on my face.

Erin leans in, resting her arm on the center console as she gives me a hard look.

"I can't be your friend. Or your therapist."

"Why not?" I ask. The disappointment is clear in my voice.

She sighs again. "Because I'm your trainer. My job is to take you to the edge of what you can handle and push you."

I swallow. "Like today."

Her proud smile settles some of the hurt in my chest. "You did really well."

"I don't understand why being my trainer means we aren't friends."

Erin's lips droop into a thin line. "Training is getting better. Growing. Finding the barriers of everything you're capable of and then moving those barriers." She shakes her head. "Most of this training takes place at the very edge of what you're comfortable with, what you can do. A friend wouldn't push you. And a therapist wouldn't let you get that close."